Dla mojej ukochanej Babci Loni.

The Storm Child is a uclanpublishing book

First published in Great Britain in 2023 by
uclanpublishing
University of Central Lancashire
Preston, PR1 2HE, UK

Text copyright © Gabriela Houston, 2023
Illustrations copyright © Alexis Snell, 2023

978-1-915235-53-4

1 3 5 7 9 10 8 6 4 2

Set in 10.5/17pt Kingfisher by Becky Chilcott.

A CIP catalogue record for this book is available from the British Library.

Printed and bound in Great Britain by Clays Ltd, Elcograf S.p.A.

Gabriela Houston

THE STORM CHILD

Illustrated by Alexis Snell

uclanpublishing

★ HAVE YOU EVER WONDERED ★ HOW BOOKS ARE MADE?

UCLan Publishing is an award-winning independent publisher specialising in Children's and Young Adult books. Based at The University of Central Lancashire, this Preston-based publisher teaches MA Publishing students how to become industry professionals using the content and resources from its business; students are included at every stage of the publishing process and credited for the work that they contribute.

The business doesn't just help publishing students though. UCLan Publishing has supported the employability and real-life work skills for the University's Illustration, Acting, Translation, Animation, Photography, Film & TV students and many more. This is the beauty of books and stories; they fuel many other creative industries! The MA Publishing students are able to get involved from day one with the business and they acquire a behind the scenes experience of what it is like to work for a such a reputable independent.

The MA course was awarded a Times Higher Award (2018) for Innovation in the Arts and the business, UCLan Publishing, was awarded Best Newcomer at the Independent Publishing Guild (2019) for the ethos of teaching publishing using a commercial publishing house. As the business continues to grow, so too does the student experience upon entering this dynamic Masters course.

www.uclanpublishing.com
www.uclanpublishing.com/courses/
uclanpublishing@uclan.ac.uk

CREATURES AND GODS

* **Stribog** – God of Winter Winds, Music and Silver
* **Zevena** – Daughter of Stribog, a minor wind spirit
* **Koschei the Deathless** – the powerful magical creature, who placed his soul in the stone Alatnir, thus securing his immortality.
* **Dogoda** – Brother of Stribog, father of the three Zoryas, God of Summer Winds
* **Zorya Yutrenna-ya** – Daughter of Dogoda, Goddess of the Morning
* **Zorya Vecherna-ya** – Daughter of Dogoda, Goddess of the Evening
* **Zorya Necna-ya** – Daughter of Dogoda, Goddess of the Night
* **Sudiki** – The three sisters in the Veeray Tree, Goddesses of Fate and the guardians of the Root Souls
* **Veles** – The trickster God of Navia, the afterlife, and the God of the Sea
* **Vila** – The Goddess of Lightning
* **Gamayun** – a half-woman, half-eagle. The protector of "half things", and a servant to the ????

- **Devena** – The Goddess of the Hunt, Vila's sister
- **Kadooks** – burrowing monsters, and servants of Devena
- **Upior** – a demonic ghost
- **Striga/Stigoi** – a demon with two hearts, preying on travellers
- **Gamayun** – A half bird/half woman from Slavic mythology
- **Kania** – a female demon who kidnaps lost children
- **Viaterce** – Wind demons
- **Vodyanoi** – Water Spirits
- **Rusalki** – Female water demons, who drown men foolish enough to approach into the water
- **Viatroduya** – One of Stribog's many children. A malicious wind sprite
- **Borovy and Borova** – The Guardians of the Forests
- **Homen** – A screeching procession of the dead, bringing death to all they encounter. Servants and spies to Koschei

CHAPTER 1

MARA RAN through the night forest, the rapidly cooling air pinching her cheeks.

Her friend Torniv, in his human form, ran alongside her, though she could see him trip and lag behind more and more. Remorse squeezed her heart. She'd ridden on his back for most of the day, before the evening light made away with his bear shape.

Torniv needed sleep and food. He needed rest in a place that was safe, where they weren't constantly waking at the smallest sound. An unthinkable luxury these days.

Koschei the Deathless was after them, and there would be no calm, no rest for either of them. They felt him in their sleep, they saw his black wings in every shadow. He was the fear that followed them every night and every day.

It'd been a year and more since Mara stole Koschei's soul, nestled inside the stone Alatnir. Since her own human soul had been ripped out of her chest by the god, Veles, in punishment for a trick she'd played on him. She would have died then had the spirit of the winds not been secretly nestling inside her immortal Root Soul.

At first the changes she noticed were superficial. Her brown hair turned silver like her mother's. Her pale skin turned the blue of frozen cornflowers. And her brown eyes – the eyes which her grandmother, Sorona Gontova, had once said were like her own, that bond of familial similarity – they turned blue as well. Mara looked like any other wind spirit now, like any one of her grandfather's myriad offspring. Pretty, pale and utterly forgettable.

For a long while those were the only changes Mara noticed, and they were painful enough. She had tried and failed to save the life of her human father. Losing him was hard and becoming so unlike him seemed to erase him further from the world. The loss of her human soul and the emergence of her divine heritage came with no powers, no magic that she recognised.

"We need to rest," Mara said, as Torniv tripped and scratched his hand against a rough patch of bark.

"I can smell water," he said, his eyes reflecting the moonlight. "It falls on the rocks, and the spray travels far. A waterfall. There might be a place we can rest there."

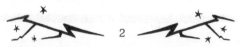

Mara nodded. She was tired too, though it would seem churlish to mention it when Torniv was being so brave. And maybe the waterfall wasn't too far, though her own ears could tell her nothing of it.

The truth was they could afford no mistakes, no carelessness. Koschei the Deathless was ever near and more than once they had seen the tip of his black wings across the night sky.

At first, Mara had thought to confront him. She held his soul in her hand, and he'd have to listen to her, she had said. But that was a child talking. She wasn't a child any more. She had seen the fields of wheat shrivel and burn as The Homen, the procession of the dead spirits, rode their ghastly skeleton horses, singing and dancing, all the while sniffing at the air, sending Koschei news through his crow messengers. Searching, always searching for the two children who dared to steal Alatnir.

Everything withered and died in the path of The Homen. If a peasant boy was unlucky enough to come across it, the skeletons would screech and scream and descend upon him, until there was no more life in him. Then what was left of his bones would stand up again and swell The Homen's ranks.

The Homen only travelled by day, as Koschei only flew by night. Mara was in no hurry to come across either of them.

She and Torniv dragged themselves to the waterfall. The air was cold, which didn't bother Mara, though she knew

it was a danger to Torniv. When they finally sat down by the water, she took off the cloak from her back and wrapped it around his shoulders. He didn't protest, instead leaning into Mara. She bit her lip. When Torniv's bluster ended there was a real cause for worry.

He was asleep within moments. Mara watched the falling water for a long while. Evil couldn't cross running water. Everyone knew that. But did Koschei know he was evil? Did the protection of the waterfall only start where the spirit knew itself? And what about her?

When Mara's human soul was stripped of her, the thing that was left: was it good or bad? The winds' natures were changeable. Did it mean she would sometimes be able to cross the running waters and then sometimes be stopped dead in her tracks, rendered blind and deaf and not knowing why?

The roar of the rapids was too loud to be soothing, and Mara found her head too crowded with worry to fall asleep. She tried to listen to the rhythm of the water, for the rhythm of sounds was what always eventually brought her rest. Instead, she heard something else.

It started as a low distant rumble. Thunder. Mara tensed. Just what they needed. Another night in the rain.

But the rain didn't come. Instead, the flashes of lightning criss-crossed the sky, coming ever nearer.

Mara gently eased Torniv to the ground and tip-toed

towards the forest's darkness. A flare of light and then another flashed between the trees.

Mara opened her eyes wide. It would be stupid to go there alone. But it might turn out to be nothing. It could be nothing and Torniv needed the rest. She walked farther till the trees became less dense, and she once more could see clearly in the moonlight.

In a clearing stood a tall woman. Her golden braids were so long that they coiled at her feet. She wore golden armour over a red tunic, though she carried no weapons that Mara could see. She had no helmet and no shield, but there was no doubt in Mara's mind that the strange woman didn't need either.

"I'm glad to finally meet you, Wind Child," the woman said. She was beautiful in the way that a stone carving was beautiful. She was cold and perfect, smooth and angular at the same time. Wide bracelets decorated her muscular arms and her eyes shone with a fire of their own.

"My name's Mara," Mara said, standing a little taller, as she always did when very, very frightened. "Not 'Wind Child'. Did Koschei send you?"

The woman raised her eyebrow. "If he had, you'd already be ash under my feet . . ." She checked herself. "I mean, no. He didn't send me."

"What do you want then?" Mara bristled at the 'ash' comment.

"I'm Vila. And I thought you might be up for striking a bargain."

"Vila?" Mara's mouth hung open. "You mean … as in 'the lightning' Vila? 'The warrior using her braids as whips' Vila? Veles' messenger, Vila?"

"All of that, but only the first two willingly," Vila said, with a sideways smile.

"Prove it." Mara crossed her arms.

Vila stared Mara down, the goddess's green eyes turning orange and yellow as her irritation grew. With her palm up, she ran her hand along the length of one of her braids, then turned her wrist in one fluid movement. What happened next was a blur of motion as Vila raised her braid and cracked it like a whip at a tree to her right.

Sparks filled the air as the huge oak was rendered in two, through bark and root, the droplets of sap charred before they reached the ground.

"Wow!" Mara watched, entranced. This was so different to her grandfather's powers, to the slow creeping of frost and the artistry of ice. This was power at its most raw, fascinating and terrifying at the same time.

"Well, you believe me now?" Vila said, crossing her muscular arms.

Mara nodded, still looking at the tree. "Oh, yes. I knew it was you. I just wanted to see you use your whips."

Vila widened her eyes.

"It's pretty amazing." Mara beamed a smile at the goddess.

Vila stared for a moment and then burst out laughing. "I can see why Veles is fond of you!"

Mara bristled at that. "What do you mean 'fond of me'? He tore my soul from me! He tricked me into believing he would get my da back!" She stomped her foot, like a small child, she knew, but she was too angry to feel shame. "It's his fault Koschei's after me and Torniv! 'Fond of me'? If that's what he does to people he's 'fond of', what does he do when he dislikes them?"

Vila suddenly turned serious. "Unspeakable things, child. Unspeakable things."

They stood in silence for a moment. Then a voice rang through the air. "Step away from Mara!" Torniv stood by the clearing, leaning against a tree to hide how his legs shook from exhaustion.

Vila took in his emaciated frame and a smile softened her features. "You have a brave friend there, Mara. A loyal friend."

Torniv looked at Mara in surprise.

Mara nodded. "She's not here to hurt us, Torniv." She looked up at Vila. "In fact, I think she needs something."

Vila nodded. "Yes, I do." She sat down on the ground, her legs crossed. "Like I said before, Veles is fond of you—"

Torniv puffed up. "'Fond of' Mara? It's his fault we—"

Mara waved her hand at him. "Yes, yes, we've covered that. Apparently, this is Veles at his nicest."

Vila smiled a crooked smile. "Indeed. In any case, though it might not have gone the way you wanted, tricking Veles is a very rare occurrence, believe it or not. And he was duly impressed. I see that as an opportunity."

"To . . . ?" Torniv sank down by the tree, resting his back against the trunk.

"To get back what he stole from me." Vila smiled. "Do you think the Goddess of Lightning, one of the two Chaos Sisters, serves willingly?" She shook her head, sparks flying above her. "He stole my golden headdress, my *kokoshnik*. He stole my ring. With the two he can compel me to his will."

"He made you his servant with a *ring*?" Torniv raised his eyebrow.

"And the *kokoshnik*," Vila said without looking.

"Sounds like you should have been more careful with them then." Torniv snickered, but the smile died on his lips when Vila turned her flaming eyes towards him and he swallowed hard . "Sorry. Yes, please continue."

"He keeps them hidden, so that I remain in his servitude. But if you find them and get them back for me, I will help you with Koschei."

"You'll kill him for us?" Mara brightened.

"Kill the Deathless?" Vila laughed. "I believe that's

beyond even me. But I will help you stay safe. And then, I will help you face him."

"And my human soul?" Mara crossed her arms.

"What about it?"

"I want it back."

Vila shook her head. "That is beyond my skill. But I will help you where I can."

"Well, I think I want—" Mara started.

"You've got a deal!" Torniv piped in. He gave Mara a meaningful look. "Don't overplay your hand. I would pick poppy seeds out of ashes right now to not have to worry about Koschei anymore. We've stolen Alatnir. How much harder can this possibly be?"

Mara sighed, her hand rising towards the pouch hanging from her neck. Inside it, Alatnir vibrated like a moth caught between cupped hands. "We knew Alatnir was on the Island of Buyan. We had help. We don't know the first thing about where Veles might have hidden Vila's headdress or her ring. *And* we're still on the run, remember? Kind of hard to look for Vila's things when The Homen is wailing and screeching its way up our trail."

"I might be able to help with that particular problem," Vila smiled. She picked up one of her braids and took off the thread that secured its end. She shook it loose and something fell from between the strands and glistened white in her lap. "The bone of a great creature. A mighty opponent."

She seemed to smile at the memory and picked up the white object. It was smooth and carved into the shape of a screw. "It will protect you both from The Homen."

She motioned for Mara to come closer. When Mara leaned down, Vila took one of Mara's braids into her hand and twisted the bone shard round and round until it was secured in Mara's silver braid. "Now, for you, bear boy," Vila nodded at Torniv.

Torniv approached the goddess.

"I understand Mara helped the Zorya sisters with her mother's silver braid. Well, here," Vila smiled, and cut a strand of her golden hair, "is a piece of mine. Its light will protect you from Koschei's eyes when you travel by night." She twisted the strand like a rope and tied it around Torniv's wrist. The hair seemed to flow and melt until it resembled a gold bracelet. Torniv bit his lip. Understanding, Vila looked at him with a twinkle in her eye. "Don't worry, when you turn into a bear, the bracelet will grow in size as well." She became serious. "But for the charms to work on both of you, you must not separate. Remember, only when you stay together will you stay safe. And the charms can blur your pursuer's vision, but cannot make you disappear entirely."

"But how will we find your *kokoshnik*?" Torniv furrowed his eyebrows.

"That, I'm afraid," Vila said, "is up to you. But now you're hidden from Koschei, I suppose you will have a better chance of finding it."

"It's not inside Veles' palace in Navia, is it?" Mara looked up suspiciously. "I don't think he'd let me back in there."

Vila shook her head. "I'm afraid not. But you have friends, little ones. Some you wouldn't even suspect. If you follow the music, you might find some of them." And with that, Vila shot up into the air, lines of fire zigzagging around her face.

"Huh," said Mara once the goddess was gone. "Any idea what she meant?"

"Nope." Torniv looked at the gold bracelet with a grim expression. "But I imagine we'll soon find out."

CHAPTER 2

THEY SLEPT the rest of the night, too tired to distrust Vila's gifts.

They woke up when the sun was already high, stirred from their sleep more by the rumbling in their stomachs than the light.

Torniv stretched slowly, the dark brown fur on the nape of his bear neck standing up as he yawned. Mara watched him through half-open eyes. Her friend was so at ease with his bear skin now, it was hard to believe it had only been a part of him for one year out of his thirteen or so. He pawed at the ground and scratched his ear with his back paw. He caught sight of Mara watching him.

"What?"

She smiled and shrugged. "You look like a real animal sometimes. Did you know that?"

"What do you mean?" He stopped scratching and turned his head to the side.

"It's hard to explain. You were just human for so long. And now half the time you're a bear. And it seems natural to you. It's like you were always like this. Does it bother you?"

"I don't spend much time thinking about it." He stood up and sniffed at the ground. He would need some time to collect enough roots and berries to fill his stomach and they already had a late start. "It's just how it is. And it's been useful, with us being on the run and all. Maybe once we're safe from Koschei I will have the luxury of worrying about things I can't control. But that time is not now. Come." He nudged Mara with his nose. "The bone charm Vila gave you only works if we're together, she said. Let's look for some breakfast."

Mara groaned and took her time standing up while Torniv pawed at the ground impatiently. She wondered why Torniv was so at ease with things. She wished she could just let things go like he did. Maybe if her transformed body had some powers to go along with the silver hair and the blue skin, she could then reconcile herself more to losing her human part.

She walked alongside Torniv, deep in thought. Casting a look at her hand, she willed something to happen for what must have been the thousandth time. A flurry of snow, a gust of wind. *Something*. But there was nothing but the Autumn breeze lifting her braids. She picked some nuts from the ground, and then from the branches when Torniv gave her a lift. They both sat eating them for a while, Mara crushing the hard shells between two flat stones.

Torniv raised his head suddenly and pricked up his ears. "How far are we from the edge of the forest?"

Mara was focused on peeling the shell shards off a nut and didn't respond.

"Mara!"

"Huh?" She looked up. "I don't know. We were moving alongside the road, about a mile or so South of it. But without a map, I couldn't tell you. Why?"

"We will have a chance to test Vila's gifts," Torniv said. He stood up, his sharp eyes fixed towards North. "I can hear the Homen."

Mara was confused. "Well, then we'd better move South. The Homen doesn't often enter the forest. Best we get as far away from the open fields and road as we can."

Torniv shook his head. "It's not the only thing I can hear. And this time we can actually do something about it."

Mara's face blanched. Without another word, she jumped onto Torniv's back.

She knew exactly what he meant, and she clung to him as he ran between the trees. The Homen travelled every day now. Every day, Koschei sent his death-bearing servants out into the world, across the meadows and the fields and the roads. Most folk living in Prissan knew of The Homen and how to protect themselves from it. They knew to hide at the first sound of The Homen's ghastly music, a wailing that could crack a mirror and split stone.

However, there were also those who had nowhere to hide or those who didn't know how.

For a whole year, Torniv and Mara had lived with this knowledge. And so now there was no need for words between them.

Vila's gifts were supposed to help them escape Koschei and his servants. They would test the limits of that magic today.

The trees were a blur as Torniv bounded through the Autumn woods. Starlings and robins, startled, fluttered out of Mara and Torniv's path, and the small residents of the forest floor scurried away from the strange pair.

Torniv slowed down once the trees became sparser. Just ahead of them was a dirt road, and over the road was a field, where the harvest had left nothing but stubble; sharp pale-yellow stalks.

"I can't hear anything," Mara said. Maybe The Homen wasn't coming today. Maybe Torniv had heard some distant farmhand singing badly after a late night at the inn. Or maybe it was the memory of fear that had pricked up Torniv's ears. Perhaps they *were* safe.

Torniv shattered Mara's hopes with a shake of his large head.

"I can hear it, Mara. It's coming. Soon you will be able to hear it too. And I can't see any houses nearby. No shelter."

Mara chewed on her lip. She looked towards the field. Among the stalks were children. Some younger than Mara, some older.

"Maybe they know to run towards the forest," she said, hope draining from her voice.

"They're too far. By the time The Homen appears they won't be able to outrun it, even if they run in a straight line."

"Then let's go," Mara said.

Torniv didn't move. "I'm a *bear*, Mara. If the children see me, how do you think they'll react? You must go alone. Warn them."

"But the charm won't protect you if you don't stick by me!" Mara's eyes opened wide. A faint sound, like the wind whistling through the ice halls of Stribog's palace, floated on the air.

"Go! Now!" Torniv shook Mara off.

She rolled off his back to the ground and broke straight into a run. The dry grass under her feet rustled. The last of the Summer sun warmed her back and she settled into a rhythm. The children were playing no more than a hundred or so metres away. She would make it. But would they listen to the strange silver-haired child? She steeled herself.

The wind changed. A breeze caressed her cheek and carried the first notes of the strange, discordant music. Mara felt the tiny hairs on the nape of her neck stand on end. Would Vila's charm work? She increased her pace.

"Run!" she screamed at the children. One, two . . . there were five of them. At least two were too young to outrun The Homen if it got too close. "The Homen is coming! Run! You need to go to your houses! Go!"

The children stopped and stared at her. Maybe they too heard the distant screeching? Or was it just her? Perhaps the winds bring the sounds to her ears only, as a warning for kinship's sake? The oldest child, a dark-haired girl, let the child on her shoulders down and turned West, listening in.

"It's The Homen! Monsters! Run!" Mara was twenty metres away now, and the children watched her with wary expressions. She must have made for quite a spectacle. A blue-skinned, silver-haired child in fine-embroidered clothes which were now ragged and too small for her. Would they be frightened of her too?

But no. Determination crossed the dark-haired girl's face and she shouted something to the children in a tongue Mara didn't recognise. The smallest child of the group climbed onto the girl's back, and the others started running East.

"Come!" a boy called out to Mara. "Hide with us! It's not far!"

But Mara just waved to him and turned back towards the forest. She could see a smudge of brown between the white of the birches where Torniv, unprotected, stood in full view.

She ran back towards him. She looked up towards the sky, where the clouds rolled lazily by as if there was no Homen. No Koschei.

The music got louder now. The screeching filled the air. Mara could see the clouds of dust kicked up in the West by dozens of skeletal feet. The gyrating bodies of the corpses, animated by fury. Fury at the living for not being part of The Homen. Fury at the world that allowed them to die and a desire to take all the living with them.

"Torniv!" Mara called out. Bile was rising in her throat from the exertion.

Torniv heard her and bounded out of the forest. He was close to her now. Relief washed over her.

A triumphant howl pierced the air. *They've seen him.* Mara reached out a hand to Torniv. Vila had warned them. Whatever veil the charm cast over them, it wouldn't work now. She glanced quickly towards The Homen and then wished she hadn't.

The leader of the procession had pulled on the reins of his ghostly horse and pointed one finger at Torniv. The rest of The Homen paused for half a heartbeat, before throwing themselves towards the running bear. Some of the skeletal demons ran on two legs and some had fallen onto all fours and kicked up the dust like a pack of strange hounds.

Torniv was closer now. Nearly with her. Without slowing down, he lowered his head and rammed into Mara. With a flick, he tossed her onto his back, bruising her ribs and almost making her throw up her breakfast.

"What are you doing?! Turn to the forest! We will lose them there!"

"The children! Look!" Torniv screamed between pants. And then she saw what he was running towards. One of the children, a little boy too big to be carried, had stumbled in the field and fallen down. His brothers and sisters were now far ahead and couldn't hear his desperate calls over The Homen's music and howls.

Mara understood. She flattened herself against Torniv's back and grabbed handfuls of his fur. She felt a sharp pang of guilt when she felt how sunken his sides were. No time to think about it. No time to be scared.

They were with the child within moments. The little boy screamed when he saw a bear charging at him, but then a confused expression crossed his face when Mara's face peeked out above Torniv's head. "Come! Trust me!" she screamed.

The boy looked at her, then looked towards the fast-approaching Homen, and reached a hand out to Mara.

Torniv grunted as Mara pulled the boy onto his back and in front of her.

"Run, Torniv!"

Torniv, panting loudly, struggled to pick up the pace.

"Can you run faster?" Mara called out.

Torniv didn't respond. He stumbled and nearly fell in the grass. The little boy screamed.

Mara looked behind them. The procession of the death-bearing corpses was closing in, they were no farther than eighty metres away or so. The weight of Mara and the boy was too much. Torniv was slowing down.

Mara leaned forward so her mouth was by the boy's ear. "Hold on tight, and don't let go, no matter what." Then she relaxed her body and let herself fall off Torniv's back. "Keep going, Torniv! Don't stop!" she shouted, when Torniv made a frightened yelp. She rolled to her feet and ran alongside Torniv, her chest burning and her bruised ribs aching.

She ignored the pain. The triumphant howls of The Homen told her plain enough Vila's charm's veil had fallen and Koschei's servants could see their prey, and also how slow they now were.

She didn't look back. She ran, the gap between her and Torniv widening. She'd never wished so much for some of her grandfather's powers. She willed the wind to sweep her up; to lift her into the air. She wanted to disappear in a flurry of snowflakes, carried soundless and shapeless across the fields to safety.

Tears streamed from her eyes. She didn't even know she was crying. What was the point of her tears? They would not sway The Homen.

The clackety-clack of bones rang out behind her like a

ghastly baby rattle. She tried to increase her speed and found she could not. Her legs were so tired. She knew they would buckle under her. And that would be it. That would be—

A howl rose up ahead of her. There was shouting, in a strange language Mara didn't recognise. Then, the shape of an old woman, dressed in skirts of orange and red and blue, appeared on the horizon. Four of the children Mara had saved were already huddled behind her, as she stood like a flame in the field. Torniv was nearly upon her but she barely seemed to notice him.

The woman's arms were raised, and the children behind her stood in a row, hands clasped, staring at the approaching Homen with a look of determination on their small faces.

Get out of here! Run, you idiots! Mara waved at them frantically. They were wasting precious time.

"Duck!" came a loud call. Mara fell flat on her face as a flurry of pellets passed over her, thrown by the woman and the children with the help of slings. Above their heads, the slings went whizzing, round and round, and another round ball of clay shot above Mara's head, hitting The Homen and exploding into thousands of shards with a loud bang.

Mara felt the small shards hit her back, piercing the ragged fabric of her tunic and scratching her. Another explosion and a cloud of smoke rose behind her. The Homen dispersed, its bones shattered and thrown to the winds.

"Come! It's gone for now!" A dark-eyed boy held out his

hand to Mara. He pulled her up, and they ran towards the old woman and the children, already turned towards the trees.

"Mara, you're ok!" Torniv bounded to her and nearly squished the life out of her as he rammed into her.

"But I won't be unless you give me room to breathe!" she managed.

Torniv stepped back, looking sheepish.

"It seems I have you two to thank for saving my children." The old woman walked up to Mara and Torniv. She moved nearly soundlessly, despite her large skirts. "I'm Mama Bohyna, and I hope you will accept my invitation to dinner this night. It's the least I can do. The Homen is broken and will not rise again today. And by tomorrow we will be long gone."

The old woman's voice had a lilting accent, though the words were spoken clearly enough. Her wavy grey hair was piled up high in a thick coil on top of her head, secured with large, beaded pins.

Mara's eyes opened wide. "You're Botrish," she said.

"And you're a wind sprite and a cursed bear." Mama Bohyna winked at Torniv. "Seems to me whatever we each are, we're friends tonight. Come."

Mara and Torniv followed Mama Bohyna and the five children, who were now laughing and whispering to each other as if they hadn't just had a brush with death.

"Have you ever met any Botrish folk? Any of your ma's

family?" Mara whispered to Torniv. He shook his large head. Mara walked alongside him, and it seemed that her big bear friend could hardly stand up. He stumbled over the roots and stones, as they walked through a grove of silver birches. His sunken sides moved laboriously and he struggled with every breath.

"Don't worry," said Mama Bohyna, as if reading Mara's mind. "It's not far."

Within a few minutes, they arrived at the encampment. Mama Bohyna's home consisted of two large wagons, painted beautifully with patterns of blue, white and red. Each wooden element carried a mark of someone's care and affection, no inch was left undecorated. Colourful rags were tied to the wooden wheel spokes. There was a cow, and a mule for each of the wagons.

"Now, you two sit. You're both skin and bone, and though I haven't enough to feed a bear's appetite, I can at least take the edge off the first hunger. Tira!" Mama Bohyna called out to the oldest girl in the group. "Get the fire going. We eat early today." The girl nodded and disappeared into one of the wagons, then emerged with an apron full of bread and cheese and a metal pot with the handle hooked over her elbow.

"Steady does it, girl!" Mama Bohyna called out to her. She sat down heavily on a little stool one of the other children brought to her. She shook her head, though a fond smile stretched her lips. "The girl insists on carrying everything in one go. Two quick trips are better than one where you drop things, but I can keep telling her until my tongue is frayed – she won't listen. Thank you, dear," she said to the girl, who crouched down so that Mama Bohyna could fish out the bread from her apron.

The old woman took a knife out of the beaded sheath dangling from her belt and started cutting the bread.

Mara was given the first slice. She breathed the sour smell in deep. She savoured the first bite. It was the most delicious thing she'd eaten in months and she closed her eyes in pleasure.

"Are they all your grandchildren?" Torniv asked Mama Bohyna. He ate his bread slowly, almost too tired to even satisfy his hunger.

"Oh no!" she laughed. A little girl, no older than three, wriggled under Mama Bohyna's arm and watched Mara with serious eyes. "They're orphans, or as good as. We take care of each other. Somebody has to." Mama Bohyna smiled and kissed the top of the little girl's head, who giggled and snuggled closer, playing with the red fringe of her voluminous skirt.

"And what about you two?" Mama Bohyna asked. She pointed at Mara. "You wear the mark of Stribog. Nobody else in this world has hair like this, nor such eyes and skin. Did you bind this bear to your service?" She tossed a piece of hard cheese to Torniv, who sniffed it and chewed it slowly. There was a harder look in Mama Bohyna's eyes.

"He's not bound," Mara said, sick at the thought. She looked at Torniv. A secret guilt squeezed her heart. Because at what point did Torniv's choice become a necessity? When he followed her on the adventure, he couldn't have foreseen how long and dangerous it would become. Torniv rested his large head on his paws and fell asleep, his large body moving up and down in a slow rhythm. Mara reached down and stroked his thick fur.

Mama Bohyna watched her carefully. "My questions can wait. For all that you're a wind child, you're a child still and you clearly need your rest. You can go sleep in my wagon if you'd like."

"Thank you," Mara said. "I'm fine here." She leaned against Torniv's bear body. She felt safer than she had in months, in this unfamiliar place, surrounded by strangers. The air was chilly, but though she was aware of it, she didn't feel it. Soon her breathing slowed down and matched the rhythm of the bear's snoring.

Mama Bohyna watched Mara carefully as she slept, but she paid special attention to the golden bracelet glistening around Torniv's foot.

CHAPTER 3

MARA WOKE up to the sound of music. Night had fallen but the bonfire lit up the area around the camp well. Somebody, probably Mama Bohyna, had placed a knitted blanket over the still-sleeping Torniv. He looked so small and fragile in his human form. Their secrets were so easily discovered, Mara thought. She lay in silence for a while, watching from under half-closed eyelids.

The children were all engaged in some kind of training. Mama Bohyna sat with two of the younger children, watching with hawk-like attention the placement of their little fingers on the strings of their instruments. The eldest girl showed another the steps of a dance, while the oldest boy was sitting cross-legged, juggling. There was a neat row of several sewn pouches in front of him and he sporadically added and removed some of the pouches he juggled with. Mara caught a breath as the boy shot her a glance and winked.

Now she'd been discovered, she sat up and raised a hand in greeting.

Mama Bohyna patted the girl she sat next to on the head and walked up to the fire. She ladled a generous portion of the stew into a wooden bowl and brought it to Mara with a slice of bread.

"Eat," she said, sitting herself next to Mara. Her tone was a little sharper than before, or did Mara imagine it?

"And between the bites you can tell me: why a Botrish child travels with you in the skin of a bear?" She pointed towards Torniv. "And don't lie to me, child. I will know if you lie to me."

How? Mara thought and a wry smile twisted her lips.

"Torniv's my friend. We've travelled together for a long time."

"Quiet!"

Mara narrowed her eyes. But then she saw the panicked look on Mama Bohyna's face and she understood. She leaned into Torniv and placed a hand on his wrist where Vila's bracelet shone.

The night became a little darker, with shadows twisting and writhing on the ground. The bonfire burned a little lower now, the flames fighting under a smothering grasp.

Mama Bohyna cast Mara a warning look and hurried towards her children who had each abandoned their work. Quickly and quietly, they all disappeared into the two wagons.

The treetops above the camp shook. Leaves fell to the ground. Mara nudged Torniv, who turned his sleepy eyes towards the sky. His whole body tensed. He and Mara clasped hands as they watched the sky turn black. Koschei's wings poured like molasses across the sky, extinguishing the stars one by one.

He'd never been this close. The Homen had seen them, and what was left of it had taken the message to its master. And now Koschei searched for them. A bitter smell settled around the camp as Koschei singed the treetops as he passed.

Mara held her breath and ran her fingers across the pouch that hung from her neck. It vibrated slightly, the high pitch of Koschei's scream resonating with Alatnir, the stone containing his soul. Mara closed her eyes.

And then, just as quickly as he came, Koschei was gone. They all felt his absence. The children's faces peeked out of the wagons and Torniv breathed out.

"Is it snowing?" Torniv said. He brushed his fingers against Mara's cheek. He looked at his hand. "Ash."

They both looked up. Where Koschei's wings had touched the tops of the trees, they had shrivelled and died, as if a fire had consumed them in an instant. The ash fell around the camp, settling in a grey powder around them.

"You will tell me everything now!" Mama Bohyna startled them as she sat heavily on the stool next to Mara. Her still-dark eyes flashed angrily, but Mara noticed the old woman's shaking hands. "Why is Koschei the Deathless following you? Why is The Homen following you? Earlier, like a know-nothing, like a fool, I thought it a coincidence, a happy accident that you were by the fields at the exact moment my children were in danger. But I'm not going to be foolish now, so don't even think of lying, wind child."

Torniv tensed and glowered at Mama Bohyna. He gave Mara a curt nod. One which anybody else but Mara could misunderstand. It meant 'lie if you will', 'lie and I will back you'. Instead, she burst into tears.

"Mara?" Torniv was aghast. He reached out and patted Mara's shoulder. He adjusted the blanket he was covered in. He hadn't had a chance to put his clothes on after he changed back to a human and though Mara had seen him often enough, he blushed under Mama Bohyna's unforgiving stare.

"I'm sorry," Mara blubbered. "I'm just tired. I'm so tired. And you're right, it's our fault. No, it's my fault. And I don't know what to do, and we have to get Vila's things, and I don't know how, and I don't know where they are and—"

"How about you tell me from the beginning?" Mama Bohyna said, gently. Her children had come out of the

29

wagons and settled around the old woman. They knew a story was coming.

And so Mara told her. She told her everything. She spoke of Stribog and her mother, Zevena; of her da's death; of her journey to get his soul back. Of Veles and Baba Latingorka and Koschei too. It all poured out of her and Torniv felt his eyes well up too. He fought back the tears. Mama Bohyna had that effect on you, making you feel like a child in need of protection. But Torniv knew there was no safety for them, not until they were free of Koschei. So he'd be hard and strong now if Mara needed to be soft. He would rely on her again soon enough.

When Mara was finished, Mama Bohyna leaned back on her stool, which creaked dangerously. She took out a pipe from the deep pocket of her skirt and put something in it from a small, wooden lacquer box. She did so unhurriedly. The children around her seemed to hold their breath.

Torniv understood. Mama Bohyna, though a stranger to them, was clearly used to making hard decisions. Decisions that would impact everyone around her. She was about to make a decision and it would be final. Torniv told himself he didn't care. How could this woman affect them?

"You're a danger to us." Mama Bohyna leaned in to bring

her face closer to Mara's. "You're also a danger to everything and everyone else in your path."

Torniv's heart sank. If Mama Bohyna was going to be a threat, he wasn't sure what he could do about it in his current form.

Mama Bohyna's lips stretched in a crooked smile. "Down, boy."

Torniv realised he had moved into a crouch, and sat back down, blushing.

"What were you going to do? Embarrass me into letting you go? Put some clothes on at least if you're trying to look threatening." Mama Bohyna turned serious again. "Now, Mara, you're Stribog's kin and none of my problem, except that you're followed by Koschei and his servants, who don't mind to whose door they bring death and misery. But you did save Manfri," she pointed to the little boy who had ridden Torniv, "so I do owe you something. But you," she nodded towards Torniv, "you're a different sort of a problem. Your skin is pale like any Prissan boy's, but your eyes and your hair are Botrish, as surely as buttercups are yellow. And we take care of our own."

"Do you now?" Nobody was more surprised than Torniv at the anger welling up in his voice. "Funny, then, that I never met any of my mother's family. It was just me and my da since I was a baby. Nobody else cared if I was alive or dead." Torniv caught a breath. He never mentioned his da, not even when talking with Mara. The wave of guilt hit him. But it would do him no good. His father couldn't see him like this, like this half human thing Torniv had become. He wouldn't understand. Far better he should think Torniv was dead.

Mama Bohyna seemed unperturbed by Torniv's outburst. "Do you think your da would have allowed your Botrish kin to visit? Do you think your village would let my people walk its paths?" She blew out a circle of smoke which dissipated above Mara's head. "No, of course not. We're all very well for the market days. Entertainment, that's what we are. But you wouldn't let a two-headed calf cross your threshold, and you wouldn't invite a juggler to your table. That's what we are to the folk of Prissan, Torniv. But we're so much more than that. We're family and, now you're here, I will protect you, if you let me."

"What if I don't need your protection?"

"Then be on your way. We're a freedom-loving people, and I would not deprive you of yours." Mama Bohyna watched Torniv with a half-smile.

Torniv moved as if to get up. "Very well. We'll go then."

"We will?" Mara looked up at him, disappointment dripping from her voice. She seemed so tired, so small, all of a sudden.

Mama Bohyna nodded and emptied her pipe onto the ground. She stepped onto the embers to extinguish whatever fire was still smouldering in there. "Very well. Although . . ."

she let her voice hang for a moment. "Although even if your ma is dead, as dead she may well be, I'll bet her family is not. And as it happens the next Khento, the Botrish clan meeting, is at the end of *Babie Lato*, as at the end of the Autumn we meet the new season together. There will be many assembled there. Many with knowledge I couldn't dream of. Maybe even some with the knowledge of what you need."

Mara looked at Torniv. "We should go. They might know where Vila's things are kept."

Torniv stayed silent.

"It's just one month, what's a month?" Mara tried to catch his eye.

He looked away and chewed on his lip. He looked back at Mara, took in her skeletal frame and the dirty ragged clothes she was wearing. A month of companionship, a month of rest. He cleared his throat and addressed Mama Bohyna. "Can we go with you?"

Mama Bohyna nodded with a smile. "As it happens, we could use a dancing bear."

CHAPTER 4

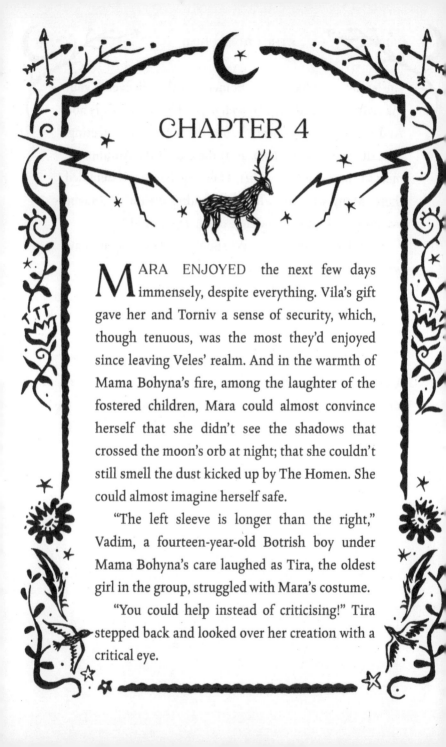

MARA ENJOYED the next few days immensely, despite everything. Vila's gift gave her and Torniv a sense of security, which, though tenuous, was the most they'd enjoyed since leaving Veles' realm. And in the warmth of Mama Bohyna's fire, among the laughter of the fostered children, Mara could almost convince herself that she didn't see the shadows that crossed the moon's orb at night; that she couldn't still smell the dust kicked up by The Homen. She could almost imagine herself safe.

"The left sleeve is longer than the right," Vadim, a fourteen-year-old Botrish boy under Mama Bohyna's care laughed as Tira, the oldest girl in the group, struggled with Mara's costume.

"You could help instead of criticising!" Tira stepped back and looked over her creation with a critical eye.

Mara shifted her weight. She didn't want to appear ungrateful but her legs were tired and she felt vaguely embarrassed by the outfits she was expected to wear.

"Are all the stars and snowflakes necessary?"

"Yes, if you want to look like a real ice princess." Tira adjusted the sleeves, which both reached far past Mara's fingertips. Mara understood it was so she could hide a great deal of Mama Bohyna's explosive creations in there.

"I'm not an ice princess," Mara muttered under her breath.

"Not bad," Vadim said, jumping off the wagon steps and looking Mara up and down. She felt herself blush and pretended she didn't hear. Even she had to admit, the costume was very pretty. It was made with a dyed blue fabric, and Cora, Tira's younger sister, had laboriously sewn on tiny little pieces of glass all over the skirt, so that every time Mara moved, it was like ice shards reflecting the light. Though not as flawless as the clothes spun from the air and frost by Stribog's servants, this dress was the most imperfectly impressive thing Mara had ever worn. It wasn't meant to be looked at too closely, Tira had explained, her almond eyes sparkling. The idea was to dazzle with the shine, the movement. Don't give the audience the time to think or consider. They come to be amazed.

Mara picked up the sides of the skirt and gave a little twirl.

"Well, done, Tira." Mama Bohyna approached so quietly

it made Mara jump. "You have created a true wind spirit here."

"But I actually *am* Stribog's granddaughter," Mara said, confused.

"It's not what you are, it's what you look like," Vadim piped in. He watched Mara with a grin. She suddenly felt self-conscious.

"The boy is right," Mama Bohyna said. "We have to make the audience see what's there. And then more besides." She put the head of the walking stick she occasionally carried under Mara's chin and gently turned her head this way and that. "You're really sure you have no powers?" she asked again. "No flurries of snow coming from your fingertips? No ice magic of your own to amaze and entertain?"

"No." Mara realised she'd been fidgeting under Mama Bohyna's gaze and she willed her hands to be still. Who was this old woman to make her flinch and shy away, anyway? Mara had faced Veles, and Baba Latingorka and more besides, and she would not look away. So she stared into the old woman's eyes. After a moment, Mama Bohyna's face crinkled with a smile and Mara knew she'd done well.

"Then we just have to create some magic for you, child."

"Do I really have to wear this?!" Torniv-as-a-bear came up to where Mama Bohyna was. Lorenna, the youngest girl of the group, was sitting astride a flustered-looking Torniv along with Manfri, who considered Torniv in his bear form to be his own personal mount, and no amount of Torniv's complaints had changed that.

Mara giggled, then tried to keep her face still when Torniv shot her an annoyed look. He was dressed in a huge vest, with a fringe of multi-coloured rags hanging off the hem and stars and moons sewn on.

"It's customary for gentlemen to dress in finery for the dances. You wouldn't want to offend your partner!" Vadim said, hand to heart, an expression of exaggerated shock on his face.

"I'm still a bear, Vadim," Torniv said. He sat with a huff. "What do they say about poking the bear?"

"Use a sharp spike?" Vadim grinned.

Mara chuckled.

Torniv glared at her.

"Now, children, let's behave. The first performance is tonight!" Mama Bohyna mussed Vadim's hair.

Babie Lato, the season after harvest and just before Winter, was a time of celebration and rest. A time when the pantries were still brimming over, and the folk of Prissan allowed themselves to forget for a moment that the long, lean months of frost and snow lay ahead.

The markets were bustling and weddings were arranged,

with plentiful feast days. It was also a busy time for Botrish performers, whose presence would, for once, be not only tolerated, but welcomed at the village fairs. Young maidens with flowers in their braids would come, giggling nervously, to Mama Bohyna's wagon to enquire about their future, and find out the name or the eye colour of their future sweetheart. Young wives would come with their mothers, all flushed with worry, to buy charms for an easy birth and good recovery.

Mama Bohyna's children would perform during the day. Vadim juggled and performed feats of acrobatic skill, balancing on an old barrel and somersaulting over a bonfire. Tira played on the *gusla*, a beautifully painted harp-like instrument, and Cora danced. Although younger than Mara, Cora was the most accomplished dancer Mara had ever seen.

"Are you nervous?" Torniv asked Mara as she waited for the signal from Vadim.

"Not as nervous as you should be. You're a bear in the middle of a market!" Mara twisted the ends of her sleeves. Torniv gave her a nudge with his large head, almost making her topple over.

"You've faced worse than a few drunk peasants," he said. "You'll be fine."

"I'm not nervous!" Mara chewed on her lip.

"You know the tricks. Just go and be the 'wind princess'."

"I'm *not* nervous."

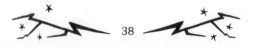

"It'll be over before you know it."

Mara turned to face him. "But it's all so *silly*! Nobody will believe it."

"They will. They've come here to see magic. They don't need much to believe they truly see it. And, with your blue skin, you're halfway there already."

"Just a trick here, a powder there." Mama Bohyna was right next to them before they realised she was even there. "Here." Mama Bohyna carefully lodged the several concoctions in the hidden pockets of Mara's long sleeves. "Just like we practised. The wide skirts and sleeves will provide the flourish, the smoke bombs and the blue and white flurry I made for you will bring the magic, and . . ." she gently lifted Mara's silver hair, which had been braided in a more complex pattern than Mara could ever attempt herself, "your silver hair and blueberry-in-milk skin will tie it all together."

"It's your turn next!" Torniv whispered.

Mara took a deep breath.

"And now, I present to you all . . ." Vadim bowed deep towards the audience, ". . . the ice and wind princess, Mara Stribogovna. My mother captured her in the fields as she sought to blow early frost over your orchards! The sister of Viatroduya and daughter of Stribog himself!" Vadim paused and mimed horror.

There were boos from the crowd. Stribog was not the

most beloved of gods, thought Mara.

"Does he have to say Viatroduya is my brother? He's my grandfather's servant, and a useless one at that!" Mara muttered.

Vadim cast her a glance and winked, before throwing a smoke bomb down. It cracked open and the stage was instantly enveloped in a reddish-blue cloud. That was Mara's cue. She swapped places with Vadim, as Tira began to play a new song, one she'd made up just for Mara.

Stand tall, Mara reminded herself. *You're an ice princess.*

As the cloud dissipated, she stood there facing the crowd. In her ridiculous dress. With the garish makeup and the blue rags tied to her hair. With the various pouches in her sleeves that she didn't remember what to do with.

Her mind went blank. The music was still playing, but the crowd was getting restless.

"She a princess or a painting?" somebody called out from the audience and a few people laughed.

"I—" Mara didn't remember what she was supposed to do or say. Her hand searched feverishly in the pockets of her sleeve. Mama Bohyna had told her how to pick the little clay balls out in a smooth movement, so it seemed a part of the dance, but Mara couldn't remember the steps now, and the men were laughing, and, then she felt a smooth cold surface between her fingers. The clay ball slipped between her fingers and fell on the ground, too softly to break.

"What is that?" A woman in the front of the crowd leaned forward.

"I . . ." Mara looked around.

"Mara, *dance!*" Tira whispered.

Mara made a few awkward turns, nearly tripping on her skirt. People were laughing now. Laughing at the pretend-princess. Tears stung Mara's eyes.

She glanced over the crowd, and somebody's eyes drew hers in.

A young man, tall and broad-shouldered, with eyes as blue as the sky, stared at her with a smile stretching his lips. The face was new, but those eyes she'd know anywhere. She felt her heart drop.

The young man brought his hand to his lips as if to blow a kiss, and a tiny tendril of snow travelled between the legs of the assembled until it reached Mara's feet. Then it exploded, a geyser of stars and snowflakes, enveloping Mara. She laughed and twirled, the frost creating paintings of flowers and leaves in the air, before pouring back into the ground.

Mara danced, not with any particular skill or grace, but nobody was laughing now. The layers of her skirts lifted up as she spun round and round, and the stars on her dress were now more than just scraps of fabric. The mirror-work on the skirt shone with the perfect, brittle beauty of ice, and she was a true wind princess in the eyes of all who saw her.

The song was near finished, and Mara remembered what

to do. With a smooth movement she reached inside her sleeve, and, with a flourish, threw something to the ground.

A cloud of sparkling smoke rose up, enveloping her figure, allowing her to slip away.

Roars of applause tore through the crowd as Mara stopped, breathless, in front of the stunned Mama Bohyna and Torniv.

"You said you couldn't do magic!" Mama Bohyna said, her mouth hanging open.

"It wasn't me! Good luck, Torniv!" she said, before disappearing inside one of the wagons.

Stribog was already waiting inside, the features he'd chosen for the occasion flowing and unstable. "I see you have a new profession, granddaughter," he said, the smile on his face not as friendly as she might have hoped.

"Thank you for your help," Mara said. She sat next to Stribog, the exhilaration of the performance slowly leaving her body.

"You *were* introduced as my daughter, and I wouldn't want the family name tarnished, would I?" Stribog leaned back. Mara wasn't sure if he was joking or chastising her. "Well, at least you look the part now."

Mara touched the ends of her silver braids. "Did you know? About my wind soul?"

Stribog laughed. "You're my kin, Mara. Humans would say 'my blood', but I don't have any, do I? So the part of me that is in you is in the wind and the soul of you. But no, I didn't know it would manifest in quite this way. Lucky for you, it did, no?" he said, as if this outcome was a mere curiosity to him.

"What are you doing here, Grandfather? I haven't seen you since . . ." She let the words hang between them.

"Before you went and got a death curse to hang over your head?" Stribog said. "So what's the plan now? I can see Vila's charm shining in your hair, but how long will that last for? Vila's patience is not infinite, but Koschei's is. You still have his soul?"

Mara nodded. She pulled Alatnir from the pouch hanging on a cord from her neck. It shone clear and white in her hand.

"His life is in that stone. Do you think he'll just forget? Or that you can misdirect him with a bit of smoke and glitter?" Stribog's form rose with his anger, crowding out the narrow wagon. "This little charm in your hair." He lifted Mara's braid between two fingers. "Do you know what it does?" Mara flinched. Stribog rarely touched anybody, and when he did it was mostly to hurt.

She composed her face and nodded. "It keeps The Homen from seeing me and Torniv during the day, as long as he's near me. It's . . ." She caught Stribog's expression.

"All it does is create a blur. It's like a frosted window. Vila can't keep you safe from Koschei and his messengers for ever, and she doesn't want to either. Let me guess,

she's after her *kokoshnik*?"

"And ring."

"And in return she will what, defeat Koschei? She can't do that, child. She seems powerful to a powerless child, perhaps. But she wouldn't stand against Koschei."

"Would you?" Mara looked up at Stribog.

The god's eyes flashed white, and his features shifted, as they always did when he struggled to compose himself. "I'm the God of Winter Winds, Mara!"

Stribog's body grew until it strained the wooden walls of the wagon. "I command the wind and frost, and I can freeze the whole earth if I will it!"

"So can you defeat Koschei?" Mara held her grandfather's gaze.

Stribog breathed out, and as he did, his body once more became human-sized. "I don't know, child." He shook his head and averted his eyes.

Is he ashamed?

Stribog stood up. "And I don't intend to find out, Mara. This is a problem of your creation. Yours and that wilful mother of yours. She didn't listen to me when it came to your father, and before that she didn't listen to me about Koschei." He paused and pressed his finger to his forehead. Apparently, without him noticing, a horn of ice grew from where his finger had touched and twisted its way up before dissipating into the air.

"What about my mother and Koschei?" Mara started. "What do you mean?"

"They were lovers." Stribog shrugged, as if this was the most ordinary of all statements. "For a while." He held Mara's gaze. "Now do you remember what I told you that day on the beach?"

Mara held his gaze. "I'm 'not indispensable' to you."

"That's right," Stribog said. He smiled, almost fondly, and held Mara's chin between his thumb and index finger so she had to face him. "You choose your own path, you forge your own alliances. But I tell you now, the Sudiki will not give back Vila's *kokoshnik*—" His face froze for a moment.

Mara grinned. "Thank you, grandfather."

"You got that much out of me, grandchild." Stribog's face grew suddenly old, the young features falling away, and the silky white beard falling heavy on his now sunken chest. "Expect no more. No god wants to be tricked."

Stribog's form vanished, and there was nothing left but frost.

Mara leaned back against the wall and sat still for a moment. She knew more than she had a moment ago. And she hadn't lost anything. So why was there this empty feeling inside her? Before she spoke to Stribog, she knew she could only rely on herself and Torniv. However, *knowing* it and *hearing* it were different things somehow.

She steeled herself, her fingernails digging crescent

moons into her palms. She was not as powerless as her grandfather thought, even if she had no powers. She was not helpless, even if he hadn't offered her any help.

She had a direction now and she would follow it for as long as she had to.

"The Sudiki."

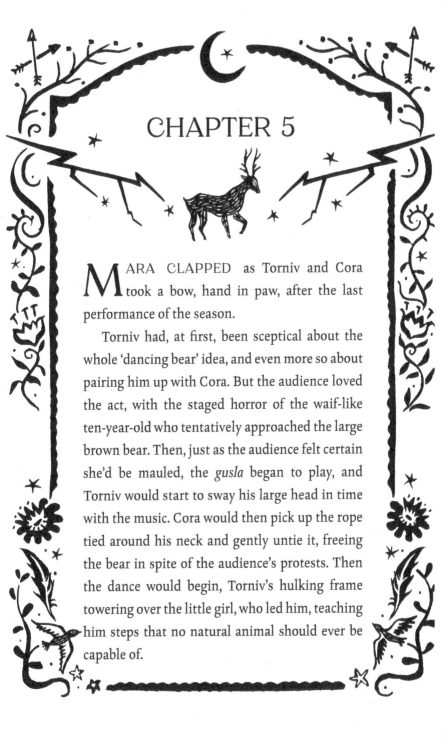

CHAPTER 5

MARA CLAPPED as Torniv and Cora took a bow, hand in paw, after the last performance of the season.

Torniv had, at first, been sceptical about the whole 'dancing bear' idea, and even more so about pairing him up with Cora. But the audience loved the act, with the staged horror of the waif-like ten-year-old who tentatively approached the large brown bear. Then, just as the audience felt certain she'd be mauled, the *gusla* began to play, and Torniv would start to sway his large head in time with the music. Cora would then pick up the rope tied around his neck and gently untie it, freeing the bear in spite of the audience's protests. Then the dance would begin, Torniv's hulking frame towering over the little girl, who led him, teaching him steps that no natural animal should ever be capable of.

Now, on the last night before they were to join the Botrish celebrations of Khento, Mara almost wished they could continue like this: in easy company, with laughter and music their daily companions.

"Botrish life is seldom as easy as it is during the market days," Mama Bohyna said into Mara's ear, as if reading her thoughts. "You're still the audience, child, seeing the glitter and the sparkle, but not the blood that went into the making of it. My blood," Mama Bohyna nodded towards the two wagons. "Their blood too," she nodded towards her children. "They know how precarious our existence is in Prissan. Something your friend will understand soon enough if he doesn't already." Mama Bohyna turned to face Mara.

Mara was ready for this conversation. In the month or so since they had joined Mama Bohyna's troupe, she herself had grown attached to the children. However, she could tell her feelings were different to that of Torniv's.

"Koschei is hunting him too," Mara said finally. "He needs me."

"The charms you've been given are little more than a veil. Unless you defeat Koschei, neither one of you will ever be safe. But we can keep Torniv hidden."

"You can do that?" Mara's eyes opened wide.

"Well, no." Mama Bohyna looked down at her feet. Mara could see the reluctance in the old woman's voice. "But there will be some at Khento who might be able to. And half-blood or not, he's one of us."

"He's my friend," Mara said, quietly.

Mama Bohyna waved her hand with impatience. "Yes, but he's not *like* you, is he? He can have a real family here: a clan, roots. With you, kept away from his family, his culture, who is he? How long can a sapling survive without the soil? You're a child of the winds. And from what you say, what little you had of humanity in you has been taken away already."

Mara opened her mouth and shut it again.

"Look at him," Mama Bohyna said. "Look at the curse he already carries for you. How much more will you take from him?" She stood up with some effort and placed a wizened hand on Mara's shoulder. "You can give him a family with us, a future. But he won't abandon you. He's loyal." She sniffed. "That's the Botrish blood in him. Only you can make him see his place is with us."

"But I'll be all alone," Mara said, hating herself for the words. She looked down and heavy tears dropped to the ground between her feet.

"But he doesn't have to be," Mama Bohyna said, walking away.

Mara sat alone for a while. Was she being selfish? She looked at Torniv. He seemed so happy. And who else would accept him as he was, spending each day as a bear? They hadn't spoken about it in so long, but had she made any attempt to help him shed the curse? No, she hadn't. She felt safe being protected by her friend, the bear. That was the truth. *She was using him.* The thought made her sick.

As if called out by her eyes, Torniv turned towards her. A grin stretched across his bear face, exposing his fangs, as long as her face. With a dancing step, he approached her and with a deep bow, he whispered, "Care for a dance, princess?"

She smiled and held out her hand.

Perhaps she would have to say goodbye to Torniv, but not yet. Not tonight.

And the children danced to the sound of Cora's *gusla*, choosing to forget the shadows.

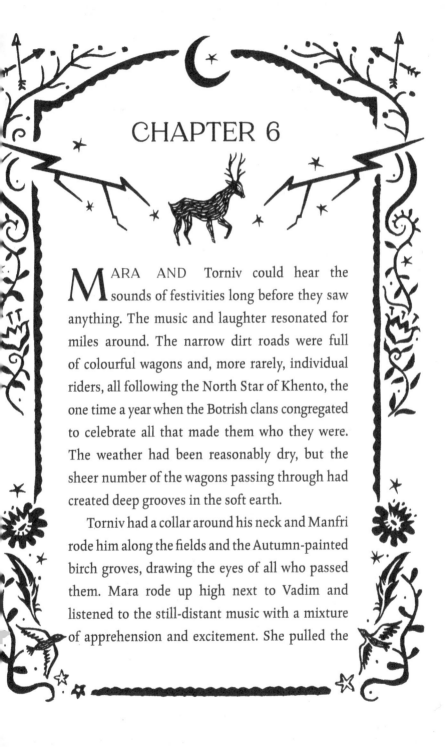

CHAPTER 6

MARA AND Torniv could hear the sounds of festivities long before they saw anything. The music and laughter resonated for miles around. The narrow dirt roads were full of colourful wagons and, more rarely, individual riders, all following the North Star of Khento, the one time a year when the Botrish clans congregated to celebrate all that made them who they were. The weather had been reasonably dry, but the sheer number of the wagons passing through had created deep grooves in the soft earth.

Torniv had a collar around his neck and Manfri rode him along the fields and the Autumn-painted birch groves, drawing the eyes of all who passed them. Mara rode up high next to Vadim and listened to the still-distant music with a mixture of apprehension and excitement. She pulled the hat Vadim had lent her deeper over her ears, her conspicuous silver braids tucked in and out of sight.

"Your blue skin will draw enough attention," Mama Bohyna had said, "and you never know who's watching and whose tongue is wagging."

Torniv didn't speak much of what he expected or hoped to find at the festival. Mara thought the answer might be 'everything'.

"Mama Bohyna!" A young man riding a chestnut horse called out. He passed Mara's wagon and trotted to the one in front.

Mama Bohyna clicked her tongue and the procession stopped.

"Sotshan!" she reached out with one plump hand for the young man to kiss. "It's been so long since we last saw each other, my boy!"

"Too long, Mama Bohyna! Let us talk properly at Khento. Will you be setting up camp in the usual spot?"

"You know it!" Mama Bohyna laughed and the young man, with a final bow, rode away.

"Who was that?" Mara asked Vadim.

A shadow crossed his face. "Sotshan. One of Mama Bohyna's orphans."

"How come he's not travelling with you?" Mara asked.

"He's a silversmith. His uncle was nowhere to be found when Sotshan needed spoon-feeding, but he miraculously remembered his young kin when he needed an apprentice and his own son took to the road."

"Didn't Mama Bohyna mind?"

"Eh." Vadim waved his hand. "Family's the most important thing for Mama. Among our folk, kin's everything. And blood, even blood that runs as thin as Sotshan's uncle's, is sacred."

Mara watched Vadim's hands clutch the reigns so tightly his knuckles turned white.

"But you don't think so?" she asked quietly.

"No, no!" Vadim cast a furtive look around, as if there were spies waiting to repeat his every word. "It's just . . ." He paused and chewed his lip. Mara said nothing, letting Vadim decide what he wanted to share with her. "Well, Sotshan was travelling with us until two years ago, right? He was our main acrobat. One day he was teaching me rope-walking, making plans with us, and then he was just *gone*." He glanced at Mara to check she wasn't laughing. He cleared his throat. "Not that I can't learn things on my own. But . . . just a quick goodbye and he was gone. And we were his family too, you know. Better than that, because we look after each other."

"You must miss him terribly," Mara said.

Vadim bristled. "I'm not some babe in need of a nursemaid, you know! And anyways, look at him, in his fine new coat with his fine horse. Silversmithing brings in more coin than juggling does. It's just . . ." He paused. "He didn't even ask if I wanted to go with him."

"I'm sure it was because Mama Bohyna couldn't spare you," Mara said. Vadim shot her a look as if to check whether she was making fun of him, but his ruffled feathers were smoothed somewhat by her earnest expression.

He puffed out his chest. "Yes, I suppose that was so. Having a man around is a useful thing."

Mara allowed herself a little smile. "Will we be there soon?" she asked.

"Yes," Torniv said, from beside the wagon.

"You better keep quiet, my bear friend! Botrish folk are understanding of the odd, but you never know who's listening!" Vadim said. "Anyways, how would you know? I've travelled this way since I was a baby!" He nonchalantly threw his arm around the surprised Mara's shoulders and flashed his white teeth at Torniv. Mara didn't like how Vadim teased Torniv and wriggled away, but the damage was done. Torniv's whole body tensed.

"I can hear the music. And I can smell ghoulash, and . . . some kind of pie?" Torniv said quietly. He seemed to always get quiet around Vadim, Mara thought. And Vadim seemed to enjoy it.

"Aah, that would be *burek*," said Vadim with a broad smile. He didn't seem bothered by Mara shaking him off and his eyes sparkled with excitement as he recalled some of his favourite treats. "Mama Bohyna's food is hearty and fills the stomach, but she doesn't bother with the fancy stuff. Too many mouths to feed, too much to do. Aah, but at Khento, Mara, you have no idea! The fried bread and beef! Nobody eats beef except at the festival, and Mama Bohyna always lets us buy it then! Even in the lean years, even the youngest of us will get a taste."

"That sounds lovely," Mara said. In the corner of her eye, she saw Torniv's ears prick up. She pursed her lips in annoyance. If Torniv wanted to feel included in the conversation, all he had to do was join in. "So what's going to happen when we arrive?" she asked.

"After we set up camp, Mama Bohyna will go to the Hedji council to see if anyone can track down Torniv's family. But after so long, if they haven't claimed him so far, they're unlikely to take him. A half-breed brought up outside the Botrish laws? Not everyone shares Mama Bohyna's views on the strength of our blood overriding everything else."

Mara's mouth hung open. She elbowed Vadim in the rib.

"Ouch, what's your problem?" he yelped, but Mara noticed he shot Torniv a quick look.

Beside the wagon, Torniv grunted and quickened his pace till he was walking alongside Mama Bohyna's wagon.

"Why would you say an awful thing like that?" Mara asked, throwing her hands in the air.

Vadim looked away. "He'll hear that and worse from others, I bet. Besides, that way you and I get a moment alone!" He beamed at the confused Mara.

She huffed in outrage and, without warning, jumped off the side of the still-moving wagon.

"Whoa!" Vadim actually seemed shaken, Mara noticed with satisfaction. She stood up and smoothed her dress with her hands before running forward towards Torniv.

The two walked in silence, occasionally pierced by the excited Manfri, bouncing on Torniv's back.

"Do you think he's right?" Torniv asked after a while.

"No," Mara said immediately. She had to increase her pace to keep up with Torniv and was getting a little breathless. "Torniv, what do you expect to find there?" She asked this in a low voice, but even so, she saw Mama Bohyna incline her head towards Torniv, waiting for his answer.

"We have to get Vila's things. That's why we're going there," replied Torniv, as much for Mara's sake as Mama Bohyna's. Stribog told you the Sudiki, the Goddesses of Fate, have Vila's *kokoshnik*. We know they live in the Veeray tree; you've met them after all. And I assume you don't really want to head over there the way you did last time. I for one have had enough of Veles' palaces for one lifetime. We need another way, and the Hedji might know of one."

Mara looked ahead for a while. She didn't want to say what she had to. "But what about your family? What if we find your mother's kin? Grandparents, cousins?"

Torniv didn't answer. From atop the slightly curved roof of Mama Bohyna's wagon, Cora began to play.

CHAPTER 7

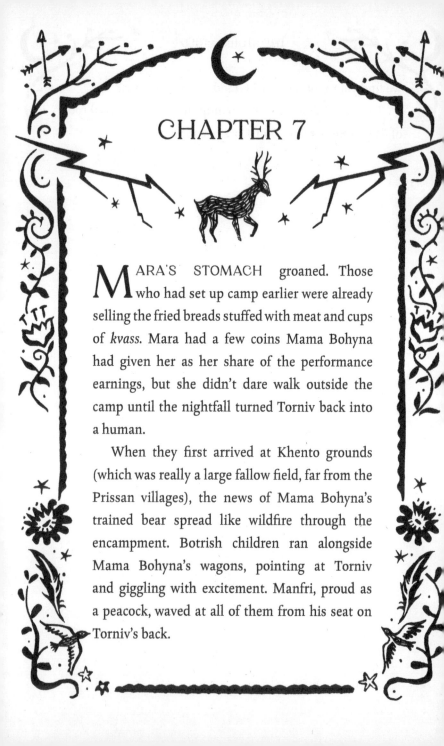

MARA'S STOMACH groaned. Those who had set up camp earlier were already selling the fried breads stuffed with meat and cups of *kvass*. Mara had a few coins Mama Bohyna had given her as her share of the performance earnings, but she didn't dare walk outside the camp until the nightfall turned Torniv back into a human.

When they first arrived at Khento grounds (which was really a large fallow field, far from the Prissan villages), the news of Mama Bohyna's trained bear spread like wildfire through the encampment. Botrish children ran alongside Mama Bohyna's wagons, pointing at Torniv and giggling with excitement. Manfri, proud as a peacock, waved at all of them from his seat on Torniv's back.

There were cages with singing birds, the tall-hatted bird-catchers' contribution to the festivities. Mara watched the mass of feathers and fluff, ready for the moment when they'd be released into the sky to sing above the heads of the celebrating Botri people.

Mara stayed inside as Cora and Lorenna lit the fire. She felt self-conscious about her strange silver hair and blue skin. Mama Bohyna had told her the wind gods were friends to her people, but Mara knew her grandfather and he was a friend to nobody, so she wasn't sure what the people's reaction to her might be.

Mama Bohyna had left for the Hedji council almost as soon as they'd arrived, and she still hadn't returned. She'd promised to ask about Vila's *kokoshnik*, but Mara knew the main purpose of the trip was to find Torniv's family. Mara chewed her lower lip, sitting in the shadows as Mama Bohyna's children all scattered in search of their friends, leaving Mara and Torniv to guard the wagons. Torniv pretended to doze off. Perhaps he was still upset over what Vadim had said, or perhaps he was worried about what answers he might get when Mama Bohyna returned.

Either way, Mara wished he would talk to her, though she herself wasn't sure what she could say.

Mama Bohyna arrived with the setting of the sun. With her was Sotshan, the silversmith they'd met on the road. Torniv had emerged from the wagon in Botrish clothes he'd borrowed from Vadim. On his head, he wore a brown woollen hat, and he had a black vest on with a contrasting panel at the back.

"You look . . . different . . ." Mara said, looking him up and down.

Torniv blushed but he didn't get a chance to respond because Mama Bohyna was suddenly standing in front of them.

"What did they say?" Mara asked.

Mama Bohyna turned her head this way and that, as if considering her words.

Sotshan spoke instead. "You'd better come with us."

They weaved their way between the wagons and the crowded bonfire parties, with people playing dozens of instruments Mara had never seen; their songs faded in and out as the smoke rose high. Mara looked up at the sky. Would she even see Koschei if he flew right above her now? The loud music and laughter grated on her after months of whispered conversations. She kept lifting her fingers to her hat, under which she knew lay the bone charm, twisted into one of her braids. She glanced at the gold bracelet on Torniv's wrist. She could just about see its outline under his shirt's cuff.

They came to a large tent. Mama Bohyna went inside and gestured for them to follow.

Inside sat two old women and a man, speaking in hushed

tones. Rather surprisingly, Vadim was sitting at their side. He exchanged a look with Mara and shrugged, as if to let her know he didn't know why he had to be present either, when there were so many interesting things happening outside.

One of the old women cleared her throat. She smiled encouragingly at Torniv, with barely a wary glance towards Mara. The woman patted a cushion in front of her. Torniv froze in place.

Mara gave him a little push. "It's all right. I'm here," she whispered. She wasn't sure if he'd heard her but he sat in front of the old woman, nonetheless.

"Bohyna's filled us in," the woman said. "She did well to bring the matter to our attention. Here, in the heart of the Botriworld, we can protect you. But please tell me, what have you been told of your mother and her kin?"

Torniv hesitated. "I—" He suddenly looked so small Mara wanted to give him a hug. He shook his head. "My mother's dead. I have a da who likely thinks *I'm* dead. But that's not important. Mara and me, we just need to get to Sudiki, make them give up Vila's *kokoshnik* so she can help us get rid of Koschei."

The old woman smacked her lips in disapproval. She leaned back and inclined her ear as the other old woman and man whispered furiously in her ear.

When she spoke again, it was with a sterner tone. "Do you understand where you are, boy? This," she threw her hand around the tent, "though it may not look like much to you, is the seat of Hedji. I'm Dorenia and we're the council of the whole of the Botri people. And a chit of a boy cannot comprehend what is and isn't important to us. So, I ask again, who was your mother?"

Torniv bristled, and Mara thought she could imagine the shadow of a fur coat standing on his neck. She wondered if he'd growl as the old woman held his gaze. But instead, his shoulders slumped down and he said, "My da said her name was 'Asena'. She died when I was little. That's all I know except that she was beautiful."

Vadim's eyes went as round as two coppers.

"Shh, there," Dorenia said, patting the boy's shoulder. "Pay him no mind, Torniv. Now, what do you know of our people and our customs? What do you know of the Botrish laws?"

"Nothing whatsoever," Torniv replied with a shrug.

There were more furious whispers from the other two elders, but Dorenia waved them away.

"You, who shrug away your ignorance, have our blood, but are not a part of us. Not truly. Not yet," Dorenia said. She scratched her head under her headscarf then looked up. "But you could be. There's more to the Botri people than what the Prissan folk see in the markets. It's a privilege to be a part of us."

"Look, what do you want of me?" Torniv said. He reached

out behind him and surprised Mara by squeezing her hand. "I never knew my ma, and though my da was kind, I never truly belonged in his home. I chose to go with Mara and now we face a threat together. Can you help us or not?"

Dorenia leaned back with her arms crossed.

Torniv held her gaze for a moment and stood up. "Fine then. We found our way before, we will again. Come, Mara!"

"What if you had kin? Here, at Khento?" Mama Bohyna said, reaching out and holding her palm to Torniv's chest, gently stopping him from leaving the tent.

"She means me."

Torniv turned round and looked at the sullen Vadim.

Torniv stared. "You?"

"Me."

"Are you my cousin then?" Torniv struggled to get the words out. Mara laced her fingers with his and his breathing steadied.

Vadim sneered. "Think closer." The boy looked up at the ceiling of the tent and made a vague gesture, pointing first to himself, then to Torniv. "We're brothers. Well, half-brothers. My da died before our ma met your Prissan sire."

Mara's breath caught. It was great news, right? It should be. But there was something wrong. She glanced to the left at her friend's face. Torniv felt it too. If they were really brothers, why did Vadim stand there like that, his face twisted in anger?

Torniv cleared his throat. "I . . . I didn't know I had a brother."

"I didn't either." Vadim crossed his arms and shot Mama Bohyna a withering look. "Seems everyone was too keen on sparing my feelings. The poor little orphan who can't learn anything, right, Mama Bohyna?"

Mama Bohyna winced. "It wasn't like that—"

"Oh, *please!*" Vadim pointed at Torniv. "The reason you didn't know about me? The reason I didn't know about you? It's because I might still have a ma if you had never existed!"

Torniv's face turned white. He said nothing.

Dorenia raised her hand to silence Vadim. "Enough. Vadim's words are unkind, even if they're not, strictly speaking, true. Asena died soon after you were born, Torniv. The Prissan folk wouldn't let her clan's midwives attend her and she sickened after your birth." She raised her hands above her head and closed her eyes. "But such is life. Your father kept you, but Vadim was ours and not his. So he gave Vadim back to us. Vadim was barely two years old at the time."

Torniv swallowed hard. He opened his mouth then closed it again.

Mama Bohyna put her hand on Torniv's shoulder. "We pleaded with your da to give you to us as well. Gods know, few expected him to keep you. A widower taking care of a newborn? He wouldn't hear of it, but Vadim belonged to us.

He's Botrish-born. It wouldn't be right for him to grow up far from our traditions. So your da agreed to give him to us."

"Yes, very noble of him," Vadim said through gritted teeth.

"My da's a good man," Torniv's eyes flashed with anger.

Vadim took a step towards his brother. A growl rose from deep inside Torniv's chest as they brought their faces close together.

"I wish the plague had taken your da before he ever met my mother. I wish you were never born. Then maybe I'd have a mother now. You were the death of her, *little brother.*"

"Vadim, that's enough!" Dorenia smacked the ground with an open hand. But it was too late.

Torniv pulled his fist back but Vadim was quicker. He punched Torniv on the jaw and set him sprawling onto the ground.

"Why would you do that?!" Mara shouted at Vadim. A white-hot rage surged through her body as she grabbed Vadim's collar. He looked at her, as if in a daze, and she saw the anger drain away from him. She froze in shock when she saw tears pool in Vadim's dark eyes.

"That's enough," Torniv muttered, lifting himself up onto one elbow. Mara kneeled next to him and helped him stand up.

"Torniv, I . . ." Vadim started to say. He was staring at his bare feet, his dark hair obscuring his face.

Torniv didn't stop to listen. He turned around and, pushing past Mama Bohyna, he left the hut.

Mara followed him.

They walked for a moment between the tents. Mara said nothing, waiting for Torniv to process his thoughts. The night air was filled with the sounds of the crackling bonfires, burning dangerously close to the ragged tents and the wooden wagons. Small children, who should normally be long asleep, ran bare-bottomed through the path, chasing a squawking chicken.

Finally, when they found themselves closer to Mama Bohyna's wagon, Torniv turned to Mara, his eyes welling up. "What am I supposed to do with this?" He threw his arms wide.

"With what?"

"This, this . . . Vadim is my brother, but he doesn't want me to be his brother. I don't want him either, so that works perfectly! But then what's the point of telling me now? It doesn't help me any! It doesn't help us! It—" He put his face in his hands.

Mara stood very still for a moment. She held up her hand and felt the breeze caress her fingertips. She took a breath. "I remember I told my mother I didn't need her. All that time ago. And then she was gone. Is that what you want? For Vadim to be gone again? Now that you know he's your family?"

"I don't care what he does," Torniv shook his head and kicked the ground. He groaned. "Look, let's just go. Right now. Let's take our things and go!"

Mara looked up at the sky again. The glare of the many fires made it hard to see the stars. She placed her fingers on Alatnir, hanging heavy under her tunic. "What things? We have nothing."

Torniv stared for a moment. He laughed. He laughed so hard that tears poured down his cheeks. He hiccupped and slumped to the ground, and his laughter turned to a sob. Mara approached him and sat on her haunches. She rubbed Torniv's back with an open hand, like her da used to when she was little and felt scared or sad.

"I won't force you," Mara said. "But we could use the council's help."

"Do you ever wonder if Zevena misses you?" Torniv wiped his tears with his sleeve.

Mara lifted her hand and kneaded her neck as she looked at the ground between her feet. "No," she said. "I don't need to wonder. I know she doesn't." She felt a tightness in her chest. "It's not her fault. She's just not built that way. She's had a long life, a very long life. I'm just one of the memories. And not even a particularly happy one."

Torniv chuckled mirthlessly. "Gods have all the time in the world but they don't have the time to worry about their own children."

Mara smiled. "Something like that." She looked away. Saying it out loud shouldn't hurt and yet . . . is this what she wanted? Her mother needing her? Missing her? *So stupid*, she thought. Wanting things that could never be was stupid. She'd kill that feeling. She would.

"I don't want this," Torniv said. "It might make our way harder, and I know it's not fair to ask you. But I'm tired of being unwanted, Mara. I don't want to ask for help from people who don't want me."

Mara stretched out. "Then let's go."

"Now?" Torniv's eyes went wide.

Mara nodded, already walking towards the road leading out of the encampment.

"We'll find a way," Mara said. She jutted her chin out.

"We haven't said goodbye," Torniv said. He bit his lip and tucked his chin into his chest. In a small voice, he added, "Don't you want to say goodbye to Vadim?"

Mara hid a smile. "No." She reached out without looking and clasped hands with Torniv. "It's the two of us."

In fact, she knew she'd regret not saying goodbye to Mama Bohyna and her children, but as they walked out of the encampment, together, she felt a weight lift from her shoulders. It was the two of them again. No long-lost relatives wanting to keep Torniv from her. No Mama Bohyna whispering in her ear. No wall being slowly but surely erected between her and Torniv. Just them and the cool night air. She looked up and grinned. Here, away from the bright bonfires, she could see the stars, and the . . .

"Torniv, look!" She stood very still, the smile frozen on her face. "Is that a cloud?" But even as she uttered the words, she knew it wasn't. A pool of black ink poured across the sky, spreading village-wide, hiding the stars and the moon. A whistling noise carried over the fields, and ash carried on the wind.

"It's Koschei," Torniv said, blanching. "He found us. But how?" He clutched the bracelet around his wrist.

Then the unwelcome answer shot in a line of fire above them. Lightning bolts, one after another, hit the ground in front of them. A path of fire leading Koschei directly to them.

"Run!" Torniv pushed Mara, shaking her from the stupor.

They left the road and shot across the fields. Then there was a flash of light and Vila stood in front of them, her golden armour looking dull and tarnished somehow.

"Vila!" Mara squeezed her hands into fists. "You betrayed us! We were going to get your things!"

Vila's expression was inscrutable, but her beautiful face seemed weary. "Did you think I could protect you for ever? For a month you've travelled through Prissan, without so much as an attempt to free me. A month where you didn't need to hide from either Koschei or his servants. Did you think he wouldn't get suspicious? Did you think Veles wouldn't notice? Well, they did and now they're making me track you for them. And without my *kokoshnik* and my ring, I can't help but obey." She looked up and sniffed the air. "Koschei's getting impatient. He expects blood this evening. I can't directly disobey Veles, but I can buy you some time. Use it well. Get me my *kokoshnik*. Get me my ring. Or you will never be safe." With that she rose up into the air, her body growing till she was a golden shadow connecting the earth and the sky. She picked up one of her braids.

Mara knew before Torniv. "She's going to lead Koschei to Khento! She's going to let him kill all the people there, to hide us!"

Torniv was running before she finished the sentence. They ran, not knowing what they could do once they arrived.

Mara saw a young goat tied by the foot to a spike driven into the ground by a Botrish family's tent and she smiled. She ran up to it and cut the cord with her small knife. With a muttered apology and a grunt she lifted it up to her arms, ignoring its cries as it tried to wriggle free.

"Torniv! Run to warn Mama Bohyna!" Mara shouted. A thought struck her. "Tell them to bring singing birds! I'll keep him off!" She turned around, hoping he'd heard her, too panicked to make sure.

"He'll see you!" Torniv made a grab for her but she was already running away from the camp, towards where a thick line of lightning drew a fire ribbon on the road.

The sky swirled and the black wings poured into the

ground a few hundred metres from her, a shapeless mound of horror.

Muttering an aimless prayer, Mara pulled Alatnir out from under her tunic and rubbed it on the goat in her arms. Her great uncle, God Dogoda, told her Koschei could sniff out those who'd touched Alatnir, even if they no longer had the stone with them. Koschei would pursue Mara and Torniv for ever.

I'm risking a lot on your words, uncle, Mara thought, as she released the terrified goat into the field. The animal just stood there, stupefied. She gave it a great big smack on the side and it took off like a shot through the field.

Mara took a breath and ran in the opposite direction. Did she imagine it, or did the shape of Koschei ripple and waver? It rose up high, and separated, two daggers of dark weaving their way through the tall grasses, one following the goat and one following Mara.

It worked, Mara thought, and she almost smiled. But her joy was short-lived as one half of Koschei reached the baby goat. Strangled bleating filled the air, and Mara stifled a sob that nearly escaped her.

She risked a look and saw the tendrils of darkness already leaving the goat's lifeless body, pouring back and mixing with the other half.

A shape rose up above the ground, its outline fluid and imprecise, except for a face, shining like a death mask in the middle. Koschei's face was that of a young man, its youthful beauty deceiving nobody. His glossy dark hair fell in a wave over his forehead. He turned his face this way and that until his eyes fixed on Mara's.

I can see you.

She felt the words in her bones. The triumph in them was unmistakable. In a moment, Koschei would have her, and his soul and all the world besides, for all she knew.

Vila...

The voice rang through the air, and once more the golden warrior rose into the air. Mara looked up at her beautiful face and imagined the goddess mouthing an apology.

Vila picked up her long braids, and she cracked them like whips in quick succession.

A flash of light blinded Mara for a moment. She tripped on the ground and rolled with the momentum, as a deafening roar travelled across the fields. When Mara opened her eyes, everything was yellow-white light and the heat made her wish she could crawl out of her own skin.

Vila had struck a lightning ring around Mara, so the flames encircled her, trapping her. The dry grass caught easily, and the circle expanded inwards, strangling out the space Mara stood in. Tears were streaming down Mara's eyes and she called to Stribog, to her mother, to Viaterce and Viatroduya and all the spirits of the wind who would never listen to her or come to her aid. The fire roared.

Mara looked up at the night sky turned red by the raging flames.

She heard nothing, saw nothing, and . . .

A blur of motion passed before her. *Koschei*, she thought, in one heart-stopping moment.

A horse whinnied and Mara looked up into the dark eyes of Vadim on the back of Sotshan's horse. "I brought the birds, crazy girl!" he shouted. "You asked for the birds!"

And indeed, in front of him, Vadim held a wicker cage full of terrified birds: the spotted starlings and little nightingales, the orange-bellied whinchats and the tri-coloured goldfinches.

A wave of calm washed over Mara and focused her mind. "Give them to me," she said.

She pulled out her small knife from behind her belt and, taking a sharp breath, cut a line into her palm. The metallic scent hit her nostrils as the red bloomed from the wound.

"You can smell me, can't you?" Mara snarled at the black sky.

She held her hand over the cage and let her blood drip and splatter on the fluttering wings, on the mass of caged terror and feathers. When she was certain all the birds were speckled with her blood, she opened the cage.

"Try to find me then!"

A cloud of birds rose up to the sky, each bird desperate to fly as far away from its fellow captives as it could, all eager to reclaim their freedom.

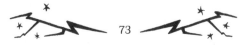

A screech pierced the air and Mara thought she saw the black shape in the sky form a hound, sniffing at the wind.

Koschei rose up from the field and, with a roar, shot out the black ropes in a dozen different directions, chasing the speckles of his prey's blood on the wings of birds that would not be caught again.

"Come on," Vadim reached out a hand, and Mara let him pull her up behind him. The horse danced a few steps before gathering up the courage to make the second jump through the flames, and towards safety.

They galloped towards the Botrish encampment where Torniv waited to bring Mara back under the protection of Vila's charm.

CHAPTER 8

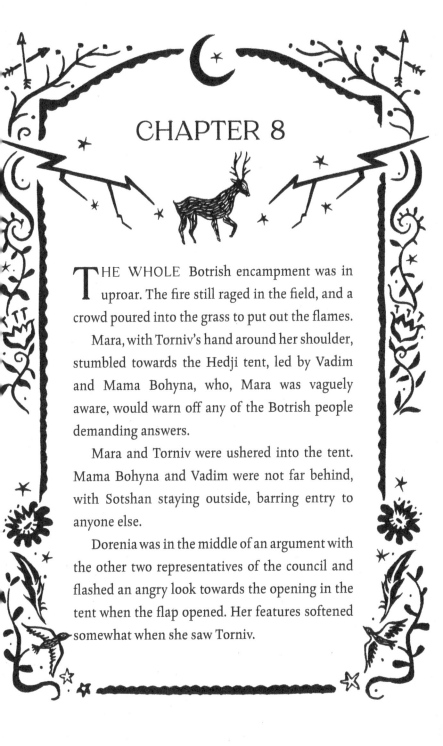

THE WHOLE Botrish encampment was in uproar. The fire still raged in the field, and a crowd poured into the grass to put out the flames.

Mara, with Torniv's hand around her shoulder, stumbled towards the Hedji tent, led by Vadim and Mama Bohyna, who, Mara was vaguely aware, would warn off any of the Botrish people demanding answers.

Mara and Torniv were ushered into the tent. Mama Bohyna and Vadim were not far behind, with Sotshan staying outside, barring entry to anyone else.

Dorenia was in the middle of an argument with the other two representatives of the council and flashed an angry look towards the opening in the tent when the flap opened. Her features softened somewhat when she saw Torniv.

"Sit," she said.

Mara and Torniv exchanged a wary look and kept standing.

"Oh, for all that's holy, just sit your butts down, you two!" the other old woman said, waving her hand over her head, so the loose skin under her arm waved like a flag.

Finally, Mara nodded to Torniv and he sat down.

This didn't escape Dorenia's notice. "So he's taking orders from you then?" she asked with a mocking expression. Torniv tensed. "Bohyna tells us he isn't your pet. And yet he put himself in danger for you, just as surely as Sotshan's horse leapt over the flames."

"If I hadn't, you'd all be dead now!" Torniv said with a growl.

Mara wondered how soon it would be for the morning to come and bring a change to his form. All she knew was she felt so very tired.

Dorenia's eyes flashed angrily. "So we should thank you then? Thank you for practically spitting in our faces, after we'd extended our hospitality to you? And then for bringing the cursed Deathless to Khento?"

"I'm sorry this happened," Mara said, her head hung low.

"No, don't be sorry, you saved them all!" Torniv smacked his knee.

"Saved us from the danger you two have brought to us . . ." Vadim said quietly.

Torniv whipped his head around and looked like he was about to say something, but he just turned back towards Dorenia.

Mara noticed from the corner of her eye Vadim squaring his shoulders. Vadim would do well to not try to hit his brother again or he'd soon find Torniv able to rip him in two once the daylight broke. She sniggered and then brought her hand to her neck as the shame welled up in her chest. Was this horrid thought hers or was that the winds speaking through her: cruel and haughty?

"Either way, you're safe now," Torniv said. "And once we're gone, you need never worry again."

Dorenia stared back at him for a moment then threw her head back and laughed, exposing dark pink gums, bare of teeth. "Is that what you think, little bear cub?" she said finally. "That we're safe?" She shook her head. "None of us are safe on this earth. Not in Prissan, not on the sea, not in any other land our people have ever crossed. We survive, but we're not so arrogant as to think ourselves safe," she wagged a finger at Mara and Torniv, "and you shouldn't either! Your charms are from Vila, Bohyna told us. Well, it was Vila who brought the Deathless one straight to our door, and she will so again unless you free her of Veles. Sprites know how you have managed to offend the Trickster God of Death, but if he's willing to help Koschei just to spite you, then the insult couldn't have been slight."

"So will you help us get Vila's *kokoshnik*?" Mara spoke for the first time. Her voice seemed strange to her own ears, small and weak as it filled the room.

A similar thought must have passed Dorenia's mind, for she leaned back on her cushions and regarded Mara calmly. "Vadim will help you if he wills it. I will leave the decision to him."

"I will go," Vadim said, brushing hair out of his eyes with an impatient gesture. "They don't know anything about anything and would run in circles without me. I will get them where they need to go."

Torniv bristled as Vadim grinned at him.

Dorenia lifted her hand and brought it down in a slicing motion, as if she'd cut through the squabbling. "However, none of you is welcome among the Botrish people, not until the curse is lifted." From Mama Bohyna's caught breath, Mara could tell the gesture carried more meaning than she herself comprehended.

Vadim led them through the camp towards Mama Bohyna's wagons. He spoke some hurried words in Botrish to Mama Bohyna who nodded gravely. They clasped hands and then Vadim climbed inside the wagon. To get some necessities, Mara thought.

As they waited, Mama Bohyna turned to Torniv and Mara. "I'm sorry it must be this way," she said, "and I'm sorry you felt you had to leave without a goodbye."

"It's not that we're not grateful . . ." Mara whispered, feeling like a thorn was stuck in her throat. Torniv moved his hand towards hers and she breathed a little easier as their fingers laced together.

Mama Bohyna looked at them for a moment. She smiled and put her hand on Mara's head. "It's just that you need each other more." She finished the sentence Mara never meant to utter, but which nonetheless felt true and real. "I understand, child," she said. "I'd hoped to give Torniv something more within our people, but like the stupid old woman that I am, I made it a choice between us and you." She looked towards Torniv and raised her other hand to his cheek. He flinched at first, but then allowed Mama Bohyna's calloused fingers to caress his cheek. "I wouldn't make the same mistake again, I want you to know," she said. Mara noticed, with a start, that there were tears in the woman's eyes.

Without a thought, Mara took a step forward and wrapped her arms around Mama Bohyna. Torniv gave Mara a shocked look. Not since her da had Mara hugged a grown person like this, not even her grandmother, Sorona.

Mama Bohyna leaned forward and placed her chin on the top of Mara's head. "When you're done with Koschei, come back," she said, "and tell me all about it. I will always have a space in my wagons for the two of you." She sniffed and wiped her eyes. "And here," she said, reaching into the deep pocket of her skirt. "This might come in handy." She placed three round balls of clay into Mara's hands, painted different colours.

"One for the sound, one for the shards, one for the smoke," Mara said with a smile, putting them in her pockets.

"Thank you," Torniv said.

Mama Bohyna turned to him. "You're angry. You have a right to your anger. But so does Vadim. You may discover you can find the way back to each other if you try." She pointed to her wagon with her chin, just as Vadim was scrambling out of it with a large pack strapped to his back.

Torniv stuck out his chin, and Mara wondered if he agreed.

They said their farewells to Mama Bohyna's children. Little Manfri cried as he threw his chubby little arms around Torniv's neck. Torniv whispered something in his ear and the child beamed a smile at him.

As they walked westward, the fires were nearly extinguished, though the smell of the burning grass still hung heavy in the air. The Botrish people they passed, their faces smudged with the ashes, shot them angry looks.

Mara put out a hand, searching for the comfort of a breeze, but all was still.

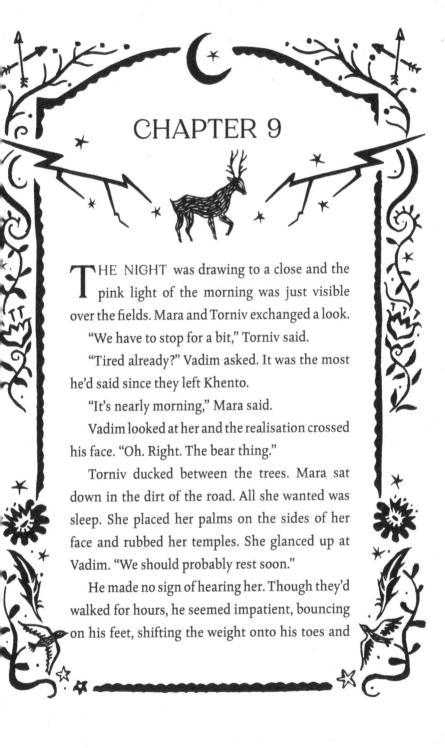

CHAPTER 9

THE NIGHT was drawing to a close and the pink light of the morning was just visible over the fields. Mara and Torniv exchanged a look.

"We have to stop for a bit," Torniv said.

"Tired already?" Vadim asked. It was the most he'd said since they left Khento.

"It's nearly morning," Mara said.

Vadim looked at her and the realisation crossed his face. "Oh. Right. The bear thing."

Torniv ducked between the trees. Mara sat down in the dirt of the road. All she wanted was sleep. She placed her palms on the sides of her face and rubbed her temples. She glanced up at Vadim. "We should probably rest soon."

He made no sign of hearing her. Though they'd walked for hours, he seemed impatient, bouncing on his feet, shifting the weight onto his toes and then letting his heels hit the ground. His hands were fluttering at his side, as if beating out the rhythm to a song in his head. He suddenly noticed Mara's serious face and looked away embarrassed.

"Why can't you two just talk?" Mara asked.

Vadim made a sound between a huff and a chuckle.

"It's not Torniv's fault you have no mother," Mara continued. A lock of hair fell out from under her hat and blew across her eyes. She rubbed them with the back of her hand. "You were unfair to him. Did you ever think how hard it was for him?" Vadim said nothing and Mara could feel the irritation rise in her. "You could have had each other. And you pushed him away like he's nothing. Well, he's somebody!" Mara stood up and squared up to Vadim. "Can you even understand what I'm saying to you?" She gave him a slight push on the chest. That finally had the desired effect. Vadim turned to her. He locked eyes with Mara, so still it made Mara uncomfortable.

He lifted a hand and pinched her chin. "I understand," he said.

Mara stood frozen on the spot and felt the wave of red make its way inexorably up her neck until both her cheeks were as red as apples.

"Hope I'm not interrupting anything." Torniv's gruff voice shook her out of her surprise, and she jumped away from Vadim as if scalded.

Vadim smiled in a none-too-pleasant way. "Just getting to know each other. You've been travelling together for a year and a half. I'm making up for lost time."

Torniv growled and rose a bit.

"What's wrong, little cub?" Vadim said. "A wasp stung you? Or are you just worried your friend might like me better than you?"

"I could tear you in half," Torniv said and, as if to prove it, he rose up high above Vadim.

"You can try, mangey pup!"

"Enough!" Mara screamed. She stomped her foot and walked between Torniv and Vadim. She pushed at both with outstretched hands, which had little effect on Vadim and even less on Torniv.

"You!" she turned to Vadim. His amused expression faded away against the force of Mara's fury. "You stop being an ass! He's your brother, and you're lucky to have him! Stop goading him!" Torniv snickered. Mara whipped her head around.

"And *you*, you big furry idiot!" Torniv looked down at his feet and sat back on his haunches. "You think I can be charmed away like I'm some hapless milkmaid from a story, with no more brain than a gnat? I'm on *your* side, always. Doesn't mean you should ignore that Vadim's your family. *Talk*." She threw her arms up in the air. "I need rest. We need a place we can stop for a while. I swear, if Koschei doesn't kill me you two will!" And with that, she strode away towards the treeline.

Vadim and Torniv exchanged a sheepish look and trailed behind Mara.

Vadim took the watch as Mara slept, leaning against the snoring Torniv. The sun was already high when Vadim shook them awake. "We need to move on. We still have a long way to go today."

"Where are we going again?" Mara rubbed her eyes. "You said you had a plan to help us get to the Veeray tree, but you've been very short on the details."

"Everyone knows the Veeray tree grows out of the sea, straight from Navia," Vadim said, cutting a piece of hard cheese and handing it to Mara.

"Yes, I remember," Mara said.

Vadim looked up, startled. "Yes, of course." He composed himself and offered another cheese slice to Torniv. He regarded it coldly, then turned his large head the other way. Vadim shrugged and put the cheese back in his pack. He cleared his throat. "But there is one being which can go to the Veeray tree at will and leave whenever the mood strikes her."

"Gamayun," Torniv said.

Vadim regarded him for a moment, possibly impressed, Mara thought.

"Yes, Gamayun. You've met her too, I take it."

Torniv nodded.

"Do you have a way to call her?" Mara clasped her hands together. "She was kind to me! She'll help!"

"Gamayun's part eagle. Eagles are hers to protect. Capturing one is the easiest way to get her attention."

"And how do you plan to capture one exactly?" Torniv was still turned away, but his ears pricked up.

"The end of Babie Lato coincides with the beginning of the eagle mating season. It takes a long time for the eagles to build their nests. That will be the moment to get one."

"How exactly are we going to do that?" Mara raised an eyebrow. "You know I might look like I have magical powers, but I really, really don't."

Vadim laughed. "Most of what we call magic is skill wrapped in a bit of show. I'd have thought Mama Bohyna would have taught you that."

"Show's all you've got when you have nothing real to offer," Torniv muttered.

Mara glanced at Vadim. Torniv's bear speech was muffled and not always easy to understand. But any doubt in Mara's mind disappeared when she saw Vadim's expression. She could have kicked Torniv. Now the whole fight was going to flare up all over again!

"I'm sorry," Vadim said, instead.

Mara's mouth hung open.

The boy cleared his throat and pulled on his hair. "What I said in the tent. That wasn't right. I . . ." He reached out an arm towards Torniv. "It wasn't your fault. None of it."

Mara looked at Torniv, half expecting him to laugh, or to lash out again. Instead, he inched forward and placed his huge head under Vadim's palm. They stayed like that for a moment.

Mara sniffed. She wouldn't think of Zevena. She wouldn't think of Yaris, her dad, or Sorona, her grandmother.

Instead, she clung to Stribog's cruel words. "*You're not indispensable.*"

She took a long look at Torniv and Vadim. *But they are.* She'd protect them. She'd keep Torniv safe.

CHAPTER 10

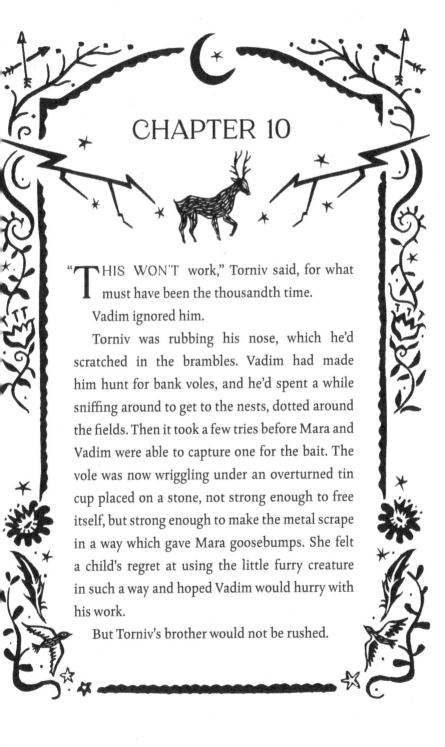

"THIS WON'T work," Torniv said, for what must have been the thousandth time.

Vadim ignored him.

Torniv was rubbing his nose, which he'd scratched in the brambles. Vadim had made him hunt for bank voles, and he'd spent a while sniffing around to get to the nests, dotted around the fields. Then it took a few tries before Mara and Vadim were able to capture one for the bait. The vole was now wriggling under an overturned tin cup placed on a stone, not strong enough to free itself, but strong enough to make the metal scrape in a way which gave Mara goosebumps. She felt a child's regret at using the little furry creature in such a way and hoped Vadim would hurry with his work.

But Torniv's brother would not be rushed.

He was building a small, elevated platform with flat stones and branches he tied together with twine.

"You sure it will hold an eagle?" Torniv started again.

Vadim threw his arms in the air. "Yes, yes, I'm sure!" He shot Torniv an annoyed look. "How did you two manage to survive this long if you know nothing about trapping? Did your da teach you *anything*?"

"I can kill a deer with a bite." Torniv stretched and placed his head on his paws. "I don't *need* to know trapping."

"Well, right now, you do." Vadim stepped back from his work. "Come here, I'll show you."

Torniv rolled his eyes and slowly heaved up his huge frame. He sauntered over to Vadim and listened as his brother explained the mechanism of the trap.

Mara smiled and, after making sure the vole hadn't escaped from under the tin cup, she walked a few steps into the forest. She couldn't put too much distance between herself and Torniv because of Vila's charm, but she wanted to give the brothers a little privacy. The peace between Torniv and Vadim was still fragile. There was hurt there, and longing too. Maybe, given enough time, the pain would go away.

She sniffed at the grey sky. There would be rain, and soon. Even the memory of the dry Summer winds had now left Prissan for good, and, with the end of Babie Lato, the Winter would not be far off. This time of year used to always make Stribog jumpy. Mara smiled at the thought. Every morning during the Autumn months, Stribog's winds would howl farther down the mountain, and every evening they'd come back, pushed back by the warmth which was not yet ready to go. And then, one day, they'd stay out, and Stribog's laughter would echo through the walls of his palace as he'd finally push his brother, Dogoda, the God of Summer Winds, off the world, and be left free to paint the fields white and the sky black. The days would grow short and the long nights would be filled with the hungry howls of Stribog's servants.

How far away it seemed. Mara played with the end of her white braid.

"It's done," Torniv said. Mara jumped, startled.

"You crept up on me!" she said, swatting at the bear's nose.

"You weren't paying attention!" His mouth twisted in what Mara recognised as a smile. Funny how, even as a bear, Torniv still looked like Torniv to her.

"Let's go then," she said, placing her hand on Torniv's head.

Vadim waited for them with a smile on his face. "Come, come!" he beckoned to them. "See here," he said, pointing with a twig to the bit of the elevated platform. "Here's where we'll tie the vole. It's exposed enough that the eagle should see it."

"Or a hawk, or a falcon." Torniv's eye-rolling didn't work as well in his bear form but he made a valiant effort.

"Then you'll just have to go find us more voles," Vadim

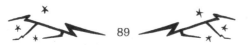

said, winking at Mara. "Watch this." He carefully brought the twig closer to the platform. There was a swish as the stick, bent on the side, flew through the air. The twine of the trap was now firmly wrapped around Vadim's twig. He beamed a smile at his companions. "Now all we need to do is set the trap and hope Torniv's nose doesn't have to go sniffing in the brambles again."

Torniv groaned.

They tied the vole by the leg to the platform and reset the trap, then moved out of sight.

For a while nothing happened. Mara sat down in the undergrowth below the willow tree, its low-hanging branches bare of leaves. The sounds of the birds circling above her head as they called on each other lulled her to sleep. Her muscles ached. She wondered if her mother's body ever ached like that. Was it Mara's body aching or was it the memory of her human form, still imprinted on her mind?

She looked at her hand; it seemed to glitter in the light. The pale-blue skin that stretched over her flesh. It seemed real enough, the pain. The fatigue which seemed to make her very bones ache. Sighing, she reached out towards Torniv and scratched him behind the ears. Mara had come to rely on him to remind her every day that she was still human, even without her human soul. If he was gone, would she still remember?

There was a screech, and a crack like that of a whip, and suddenly a bird, nearly as big as Mara, was struggling at the end of Vadim's twine. The eagle's white and grey feathers reflecting the sunlight.

"We got it!" Torniv whooped. They all rushed over to the bird.

"Wonderful," Mara said, scratching her head as they watched the furious bird. "Now what?"

"Now," Vadim grinned, "we call Gamayun."

CHAPTER 11

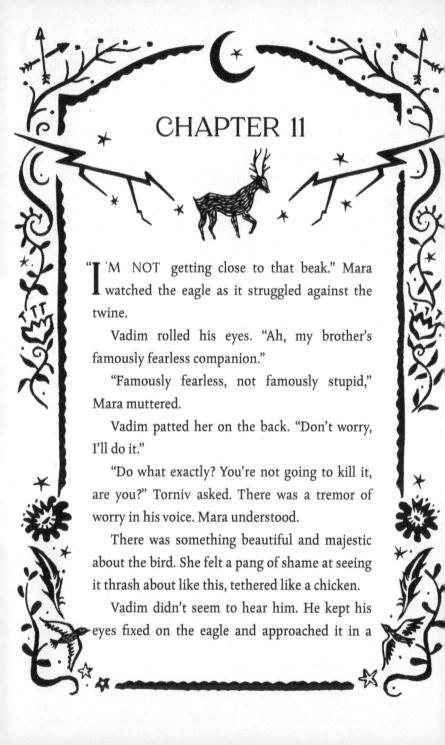

"I'M NOT getting close to that beak." Mara watched the eagle as it struggled against the twine.

Vadim rolled his eyes. "Ah, my brother's famously fearless companion."

"Famously fearless, not famously stupid," Mara muttered.

Vadim patted her on the back. "Don't worry, I'll do it."

"Do what exactly? You're not going to kill it, are you?" Torniv asked. There was a tremor of worry in his voice. Mara understood.

There was something beautiful and majestic about the bird. She felt a pang of shame at seeing it thrash about like this, tethered like a chicken.

Vadim didn't seem to hear him. He kept his eyes fixed on the eagle and approached it in a low crouch, his palms in front of him. The eagle stopped moving and turned its head to the side, better to see the approaching boy. Mara held her breath.

Everything seemed to happen all at once. Vadim moved to the right, and the eagle leapt forward, its golden beak ready to tear into its captor's face.

Vadim twirled around, and he quickly grabbed the twine tied to the eagle's leg. He lifted the bird upside down and pulled one long tail feather out.

The eagle screeched in outrage but Vadim held it well away from his body. He held the feather in his teeth and pulled out a knife.

"No! Don't!" Mara screamed.

A flash of metal as Vadim cut the twine and the eagle was free.

Vadim took the feather from between his teeth and gave Mara a triumphant look.

"What did you think I was going to do? Killing an eagle would be as helpful in getting us Gamayun's help as burning a cow would be in making cheese," he said. He waved the long feather in front of the girl's face. "This, we need."

Vadim sat down on the rock where the eagle trap had been, first sweeping away the remains of it with his hand. He rummaged through the pack he'd brought and pulled out a long yellow candle. He held it to his nose.

"Mmm, wasting Mama Bohyna's good candle on you

two." He wiggled an eyebrow. Mara could smell the beeswax from two paces away. The smell of honey and sunshine, as sweet and comforting as her grandmother Sorona's porridge. She pushed the feeling down.

"It's good we've had dry weather this month," Vadim said, "otherwise this next bit would be a little trickier." He tied a bit of string around the feather, leaving just a small piece sticking up at the tip. He picked up a handful of yellowing grass and arranged it in a little heap in front of him. Then he took a tinderbox out of his pack. A scrape and a spark and a small fire burned in front of him. Vadim lit the candle and passed it to Mara.

"Now, wind princess, drip the wax onto the feather," he said.

Torniv came up to them, curiosity twinkling in his eyes.

"Don't look at him, look at the candle," Vadim said to Mara. He turned the feather around, holding onto each tip, as if it was a piece of roasted meat.

Mara turned her attention back to her task, and slowly, drop by drop, they covered the entire feather.

Vadim blew on it as the wax solidified and then held it up against the light.

Mara must have looked doubtful, for the boy laughed. "I know it looks like a sorry waste of a pretty feather, but it should work."

"How do you know all this?" Torniv asked.

"Oh, you know, just the magical, mystical ways of our people," Vadim said, making a vague gesture above his head. He winked at Mara. Mara wished he wouldn't do that, as she could sense Torniv tensing next to her.

"So what do we do now?" Torniv asked.

"We wait." Vadim put the feather away and stretched out in the grass, placing his pack below his head. He folded his arms over his face, seemingly as relaxed as if they'd come to a picnic.

"Wait for what?" Mara glanced up at the sky.

"Are you scared of being still for a moment because of our deathless friend or because of the wind-god blood in you?" Vadim muttered without looking at her.

Mara sucked in a sharp breath. Was she really so like her grandfather now? Never mind. She'd worry about that later. "If you think it's sensible to sit around waiting for Koschei or The Homen to find us, then go ahead. I'd rather live a little longer, thank you very much!"

"Gamayun can carry two kids but unless you're planning on leaving my brother here, don't you think he needs to be a bit less, well, bear-sized?" Vadim said.

"Oh."

"Yes, 'oh'. Now the two of you can stop hovering over me like flies over manure and just relax already. Take a nap. Eat. You might not get another chance."

"He has a point." Torniv nudged Mara with his nose. "Try to rest."

GABRIELA HOUSTON

When the evening light lay low on the fields, Torniv stretched with a yawn that could take the head off a deer and trotted towards the privacy of the trees with his clothes in his jaws.

As soon as Torniv was out of earshot, Vadim turned to Mara. "So, say you get Vila's things. Say you somehow get rid of Koschei the Deathless. What then?"

"That's assuming an awful lot," Mara said. She eyed Vadim warily.

He leaned forward, his folded hands hanging between his knees. "Are you going to live with Stribog? Because I can't see you content to move back with your grandmother and live a peasant woman's life."

Mara opened her mouth. Then closed it again. "Don't assume you know me," she said, with as much ice in her voice as she could muster. Perhaps if her words were withering enough, Vadim wouldn't ask her any other questions she didn't know the answers to.

"Are you going to travel with us? Grow to be a Botrish wife to a boy who's a bear half the time?" Vadim's dark eyes twinkled with curiosity. "Or maybe a wife to his charming older brother?"

Mara pursed her lips. He was *enjoying* this.

He cocked his head to the side. "Either way, Torniv's

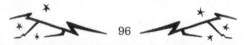

96

place is with us. You know this. He got himself cursed for your sake. There aren't many places that will accept a cursed soul like his."

Not this again. "Torniv can make up his own mind," she said.

"Except he won't. He wants you to make it up for him," Vadim said.

"Thanks for that," Torniv said, as he emerged from between the trees, pulling his tunic over his head. "Mara can choose whatever she wants to do," he said, without looking at her, "and when she does, I'll be there."

"You're half Botrish," Vadim said. "You belong with us."

"I know who I am." Torniv's voice was gruff, same as it always was straight after a transformation, as if he was getting used to the different shape of his throat. "I don't need anybody to tell me who to be or where to be or how to be."

"You're still a child." Vadim made a vague gesture. "You don't know what you don't know."

Torniv flashed his teeth in a snarl. "I'm the child whose bones break and regrow into a different shape every morning and night. I'm the child who's faced monsters and gods and giant serpents, and I did all that with Mara, so don't you dare tell her I don't belong with her!" He straightened up, as if suddenly aware of what he'd just said. A blush coloured his cheeks. "Anyway," he said, turning his face away, "let's get through this first. No point in worrying about the weave of the cloth before you've bought the lamb."

"Sounds like a plan," Mara said, hoping her voice didn't break.

"Very well." Vadim pulled the waxed feather out of his bag. "Let's do this." He scratched his head. "First, Torniv, I need you to stand on one leg while I light the feather."

"Why?" Torniv narrowed his eyes.

"Do *you* know how to call Gamayun?"

"No."

"Then on to one leg you hop."

Torniv lifted one leg like a stork. He kept his face carefully blank, in the hope it could help him preserve a little of his dignity. Vadim lit the feather and held it up above his head.

"It stinks!" Mara wrinkled her nose.

"It's still just a burning feather." Vadim waved it above his head. "Right, Torniv, I need you to spin around, on one leg, and wave your right arm above your head."

Torniv began to spin, but then stopped the moment he lifted his arm. "You're having a laugh at my expense, aren't you?"

Vadim grinned. "It's what brothers are for, I hear."

Torniv glared, but Mara began to laugh.

"Oh, you think it's funny, do you?" Torniv made a face and hopped towards Mara on one leg, waving his arms in the air.

"Don't forget the pirouetting!" Vadim said.

Torniv nodded sagely. "Of course, of course, my apologies. Shouldn't forget the pirouetting. Very important, that!" And he spun like a dancer at a Tsar's banquet.

Whether it was the sight of Torniv hopping or the relief that it was still possible to laugh and be silly, even after everything, it was hard to tell. But Mara bent over with laughter and a smile broke across Torniv's face, and the three of them laughed until tears were pouring down their faces.

"Let me in on the joke?" A voice came from above them.

"Oh..." Mara lifted her face to the sky. "Hello, Gamayun."

CHAPTER 12

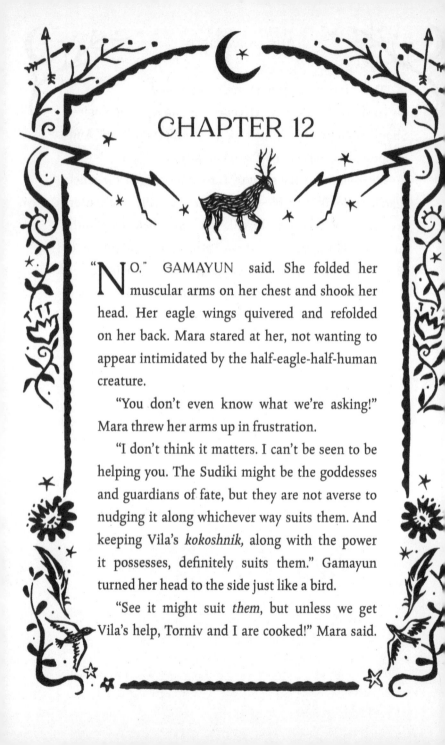

"NO." GAMAYUN said. She folded her muscular arms on her chest and shook her head. Her eagle wings quivered and refolded on her back. Mara stared at her, not wanting to appear intimidated by the half-eagle-half-human creature.

"You don't even know what we're asking!" Mara threw her arms up in frustration.

"I don't think it matters. I can't be seen to be helping you. The Sudiki might be the goddesses and guardians of fate, but they are not averse to nudging it along whichever way suits them. And keeping Vila's *kokoshnik,* along with the power it possesses, definitely suits them." Gamayun turned her head to the side just like a bird.

"See it might suit *them*, but unless we get Vila's help, Torniv and I are cooked!" Mara said.

"You know Koschei hunts us! You know that, unless we find a way out of this, he will eventually catch up to us!"

Was that shame on Gamayun's face? She shook her head and the waves of her red hair lifted up like a cloud. "I am sorry for that, but I can't interfere. It's not simply a favour you ask of me. If I help you, there will be a great deal of anger, and a lot of it will be directed at me and those I protect."

"I heard you say once that 'half things are yours to protect'!" Mara pointed at Gamayun. "Well, that's me, and that's Torniv in more ways than one! What have you done to protect us?"

"I'm sorry, wind child," Gamayun shook her head. "If you two find your way up the Veeray tree, it will not be with me." She stretched her wings and bounced on the branch.

Mara's heart sank.

The ground rumbled beneath their feet. Long ridges appeared in the soil, like a plough was working it from beneath.

"What is that?" Vadim screamed.

"I was going to ask you!" Torniv said, turning so he was back-to-back with Mara, who pulled out her knife. *A small, useless thing*, she thought. *Just like you*. The words came unbidden. She steeled herself.

The dry soil cracked and broke, and, from beneath the earth, a face appeared, with filmy, unseeing eyes and a mouth too full of sharp teeth to close. Tiny, misshapen

GABRIELA HOUSTON

hands helped the creature push itself up, and the rest of its body slithered out from the soil, ringed like an earthworm, pink and slick, the long body contracting and elongating rhythmically.

"What is that?" Mara said, leaning harder against Torniv's back.

"Kadooks," Gamayun said from above. "Devena's servants."

"Devena? The Goddess of the Hunt? Why?" Vadim picked up a branch and waved it in a long arch, aiming it at two more creatures slithering out of the ground next to him. The kadooks just sniffed the air and evaded the blow with a sway of their pale bodies.

Torniv screamed. A tail poked out of the ground and wrapped itself around his ankle, pulling him under.

"No!" Mara stuck her knife into the kadook's flesh. Green liquid oozed under her fingers as the creature thrashed about. A muffled screech came from under the soil and Torniv was free.

A sharp pain shot through Mara, as another kadook sank its needle-like teeth into her shoulder. She felt some of the teeth snap as they ripped into her muscle and felt the heat of the creature's breath. Sick rose up in her throat.

Somebody, it must have been Torniv, slammed into her and stabbed the kadook in its film-covered eyes. Mara screamed as the creature's teeth broke off in her shoulder with a sickening crunch. She toppled onto Torniv. They both fell hard. Mara looked up and, in the haze, saw a twisting mass of the giant creatures rising in front of them.

Vadim, screaming, threw himself into the fray, slashing with his knife, kicking and stomping, as more and more kadooks slithered out of the ground.

Mara tried to get up, but her vision blurred and her legs refused to lift her.

She looked down at the ground and into Torniv's worried eyes. "I'm ok," she said. She tried standing again, and she must have succeeded, for the dry earth was first centimetres from her face and then her body lifted and the dust was no longer in her eyes.

She squinted. Torniv was standing too, yet his face was below her looking up.

She looked at her feet, dangling above the ground.

She opened her mouth to scream. What she had taken for the wind was the flapping of Gamayun's wings as she lifted Mara above the fray, higher and higher.

"No!" Mara screamed and tried wriggling out of Gamayun's talons, which sent a current of pain through her injured shoulder. "Torniv! He's still there! He needs me! Gamayun, let me down! Let me down!"

"I'm sorry," Gamayun said. "Letting down mortals is in fact what we do, little Mara. You will learn."

"No!" Mara's hand ran to her braid, and she twisted

out Vila's charm. "Torniv! Catch!" she screamed, throwing
the bone charm towards Torniv. He looked up and nodded,
and then he disappeared from view.

CHAPTER 13

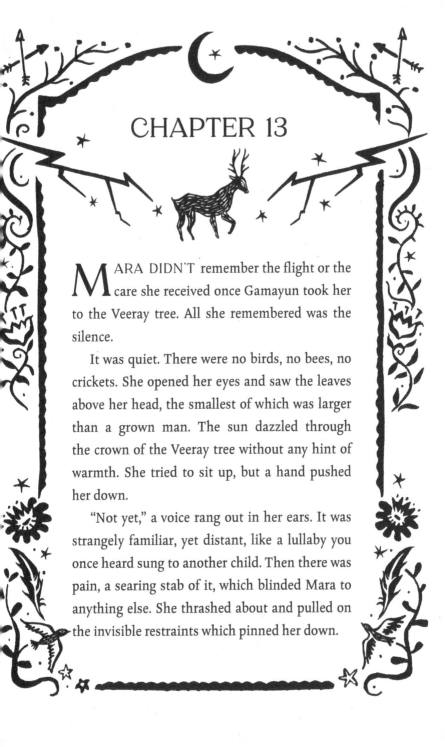

MARA DIDN'T remember the flight or the care she received once Gamayun took her to the Veeray tree. All she remembered was the silence.

It was quiet. There were no birds, no bees, no crickets. She opened her eyes and saw the leaves above her head, the smallest of which was larger than a grown man. The sun dazzled through the crown of the Veeray tree without any hint of warmth. She tried to sit up, but a hand pushed her down.

"Not yet," a voice rang out in her ears. It was strangely familiar, yet distant, like a lullaby you once heard sung to another child. Then there was pain, a searing stab of it, which blinded Mara to anything else. She thrashed about and pulled on the invisible restraints which pinned her down.

Then gradually, the pain receded, leaving her shoulder cold and oddly numb.

Mara closed her eyes and slowed her breath. The smell of the cold surrounded her, bursting the small blood vessels in her nose. Most people didn't know that cold had a smell. But for Mara, it held the scent of her life. She didn't even need to look. "Mother."

Zevena stroked Mara's forehead, pushing away a strand of hair. "You're awake," she said. "That's good."

Mara turned her face towards her mother. A sense of longing squeezed her heart. Zevena looked just the same. The same silver hair. The same face, as smooth and expressionless as porcelain. "You healed me," she said.

"You healed yourself, granddaughter," Stribog's voice whistled through the leaves in an endless echo.

A snowflake fell on Mara's nose, and remained there, unmelted. She sat up and saw a whirlwind twist its way along the branch, growing until it solidified into one of her grandfather's many forms.

"I can't do that," Mara said. There was an ashen taste in her mouth and a sinking feeling in her chest.

Stribog's face remained impassive. "If you say so."

"Torniv!" A thought pierced through the fog of Mara's mind. "He was left there! He and Vadim! We have to help them! Gamayun!" She stood up on shaky legs. "Gamayun, you have to take me back! Torniv needs me!"

"You've been a guest here for two days and nights," Zevena said. "Your friend has either found his way from the kadooks or not. Either way, he doesn't need you at this moment."

Mara whipped her head around and stared up at her mother's face. "And you're the expert on the subject, I take it?" She tried to keep the old resentment down, but the words poured out all the same. "You couldn't wait to abandon me, so I should abandon Torniv? What are you even doing here?"

Zevena's brow wrinkled slightly. Mara took it as a victory.

"Gamayun has sent us a message. You have put her in an awkward position, and so we have come to investigate." Stribog folded his arms on his chest. It was as if he was scolding her. "You are of the winds and so my responsibility, as far as the gods and creatures of Veeray are concerned."

Mara gritted her teeth. He had no right! "I don't have the time to sit here and talk to you two!" She turned away, trying to peer between the branches. "Gamayun, where are you?"

"You don't have the time?" Stribog's form shifted and grew, until he towered over Mara. "*You*, the least of my kin, think you can dismiss me like I'm the memory of last year's frost?"

Mara folded her arms and narrowed her eyes. Even if her grandfather grew to be as tall as a mountain or as wide as a river, she would no longer fear him. "You've told me over and again, I mean nothing to you. That you would not help me. That you didn't care. Well, then why should I care about you?" She lifted a finger and pointed it at Stribog and her mother. "I don't need you any more! Go to your ice palaces, your home, so undeserving of the name, and leave me be!

"That is what you wanted, mother, isn't it?"

A tear rolled down Mara's cheek. She wiped it away with her sleeve and glared at her mother, as if challenging Zevena to mention it. Mara's beautiful mother. Who never hugged or comforted her daughter. *She had no right to intervene now. No right to come here and pretend to care.* When Mara's da died, Zevena couldn't wait to get away. Away from the messy human feelings. "So now you're here to, what? Give me motherly advice? Sing me a lullaby?" She made a cutting gesture, as if she wished to cut the bond between herself and the stricken-looking Zevena. "Just go back to your bloodless life! To being the nothing you were before my father met you! You know he was the best of you and now he's gone. And I don't need what's left!"

Zevena's hand flew to her mouth. She looked almost . . . ashamed? Was that even possible? "You're angry." Zevena frowned as if trying to solve a particularly challenging riddle. "But you said . . . you told me you didn't need me."

Mara threw her arms in the air. "I was *eleven*! My father had just died and I was going to save him and you needed *me* to tell *you* that I needed my mother?" She stood there, her chest rising and falling as she struggled to contain her anger. There were no sounds but the echoing of their voices between the branches. *How could a 'tree of life' be so lifeless?*

Mara covered her eyes with one hand. What was the point? She looked again at her mother, her beautiful icicle of a mother. "I don't have the time for this," she said. "I need Vila's *kokoshnik*. I need to save Torniv. I need to get Koschei off our backs."

Zevena winced.

Mara chuckled mirthlessly. "Oh yes. I almost forgot. You and Koschei have a history, don't you?" She nodded to Stribog who sat on a branch, apparently lost in thought. "Grandfather told me. And Gamayun once mentioned it too." She looked at Zevena's stricken face. "So it's true? Well, unless I find a way out of this, then your lover will kill me soon enough. And you won't have to worry any more about whether I need you or not."

"Devena has your friend. His brother too," Stribog said suddenly.

Mara hid her surprise. She faced her grandfather. "What would the Goddess of the Hunt want with us? Have I offended another god somehow?"

For a god of wind, Stribog remained almost unnaturally still. His eyes were fixed on Mara. "She has Vila's ring," he said.

Mara's eyes went wide. Her fingers dug into the bark of the branch beneath her.

Stribog nodded. "And she doesn't want to part with it. Veles must have warned her."

"Torniv . . ." Mara put her face in her hands. "She has Torniv."

"It's disappointing to see you care, granddaughter of mine." Stribog turned his face to the side and another face grew out of his cheek. It felt like he was looking at Mara from different angles at the same time. "And surprising." Suddenly he smacked his knees and laughed. "I like surprises!"

Mara felt rage fill her chest. Her hands rolled into fists and she was moving before she knew it.

The punch flew harmlessly through the air as Stribog's form dissipated. Mara swore as a crushing sensation enveloped her. A formless cloud surrounded her body, immobilising her. It suspended her in mid-leap, her arm curved in the punch she threw.

"No kin or child of mine has ever tried to strike me before . . . " Mara struggled against the hold Stribog had on her. "And no god has ever dared."

He was going to crush her. A shiver ran down her spine as the reality of the situation hit her. *He would pull the air out of her lungs or drown her in her blood. Or just turn her into an ice statue to warn others who'd be stupid enough to try to hit a god.*

She closed her eyes and waited for the pain to start. Instead, she felt a soft pressure, like a dozen arms were embracing her. "Your human friends are alive. Devena is the

Goddess of the Hunt, after all. And you are the prized prey, child," a whisper tickled her ear. Then the pressure eased and her body fell down gracelessly.

"Ouch!" Mara massaged her scraped knee. She glanced up to see Zevena's face. "Oh, what do you want from me? Shouldn't you be leaving with grandfather now?"

"There are things you don't know," Zevena said, "but I suppose it's my fault for not telling you. There are things I don't understand." She looked up thoughtfully. "But I suppose that's my fault too, for not taking the pains to learn." She seemed so out of place, this wind spirit in the lushness of the Veeray tree. Zevena knelt next to Mara and placed her hands on her startled daughter's cheeks. She leaned forward and kissed Mara's forehead. A chill ran like a current across Mara's skin and, just like that, her mother was gone.

Mara stood up on shaky legs and looked around her. "Sudiki!" she called out. Nothing happened. "Of course, why would they show when called," she muttered under her breath, and set out along the twisted branches.

CHAPTER 14

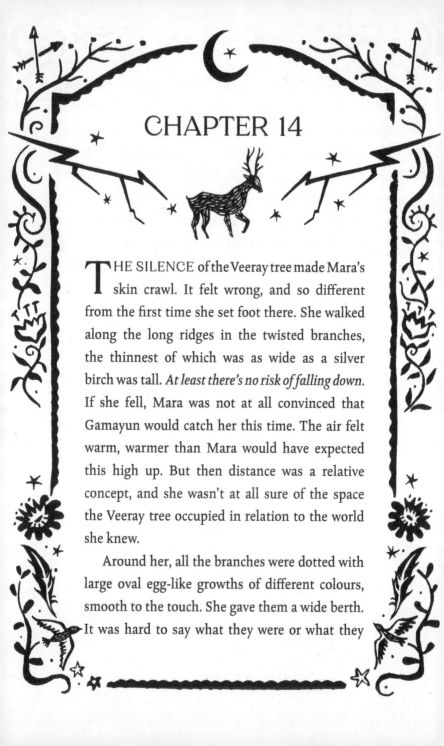

THE SILENCE of the Veeray tree made Mara's skin crawl. It felt wrong, and so different from the first time she set foot there. She walked along the long ridges in the twisted branches, the thinnest of which was as wide as a silver birch was tall. *At least there's no risk of falling down.* If she fell, Mara was not at all convinced that Gamayun would catch her this time. The air felt warm, warmer than Mara would have expected this high up. But then distance was a relative concept, and she wasn't at all sure of the space the Veeray tree occupied in relation to the world she knew.

Around her, all the branches were dotted with large oval egg-like growths of different colours, smooth to the touch. She gave them a wide berth. It was hard to say what they were or what they were for, and surprises tended to bring nothing good in Mara's recent experience.

She came up to what she assumed was the central trunk. She placed her hand on the ridge of it and pulled at it, trying to peel away the bark. Mara had no idea what drove her, except she couldn't stop herself. Her arms and back tensed as she pulled. It didn't budge.

That was it.

She was going mad.

She stared at the reddish brown of the trunk in front of her and carefully, gingerly, placed her hand on it again.

Under her skin, the tree's life flowed and murmured as the thick sap circulated in a steady rhythm. The tree itself expanded and contracted almost imperceptibly under her palm, in an unmistakable pattern. *But how . . . ?*

She'd climbed the Veeray tree once before. She had scraped and calloused her hands along the folds of the tree's trunk, as she made her way up from Navia in pursuit of her father's immortal Root Soul. She had felt nothing then, but the rough bark under her fingers. So why now?

But there was one thing different in her now. She looked down at the sky-blue skin of her hands. Her human part was gone. But why would she be able to sense this lifeforce pulsating through the Veeray tree? She'd thought of her wind heritage as a lack. A lack of human warmth, lack of feeling. Her grandfather brought Winter and cold and death, never life. So why did she feel this rhythm of the tree of life in her very bones?

She closed her eyes and took a deep breath. This was not important. This was a thought for another day.

She thought of her father and let in the pain of the memory of her loss. Losing her link to him made her less than she was, not more. She had to remember that and remember him. She took her hand away from the tree. She was Yaris Gontovy's daughter and not some wind sprite, with their small meaningless powers and even smaller hearts.

She straightened herself up. If the Sudiki were going to avoid her, she'd have to find a way to get their attention.

Gamayun had come when Vadim caught the eagle and burned its feather.

Sudiki were the guardians of fate, tied to the tree of life. Mara took out her knife. She knelt down and felt the surface of the tree under her fingers. She found the ridge of one section of the bark, like a scale of some mythical serpent, and she jammed her knife under it.

The knife was small and the bark was thick and hard. Mara's hands were badly scratched and bleeding by the time she managed to loosen the first section. She thought it felt as heavy as a boulder as she heaved it aside, revealing the smooth surface underneath. It was unlike any type of wood she'd ever seen before, pale red and glistening. The edges of the hole she had made were already releasing sticky sap to heal the wound, as sticky and sweet-smelling as honey. Mara strongly suspected she should not allow herself to be stuck in it, lest she became like the insects trapped in amber that were collected off the shores of the Prissan sea.

She had to work fast. She stabbed at the hard wood with her knife, driving it into a single space until she managed to splinter off a sliver of the wood, no larger than a sparrow's wing. She picked it up and raised it against the sun. It was wood in the same way that diamond was rock. It shimmered in the light, sticky from the sap, luminescent in Mara's palm.

Mara sat away from the hole she'd made and smelled the splinter she'd managed to chip off. It had a sweet, heavy scent, which made her head spin. She felt so hungry, and the wood sparkled in her hand. It was light and smelled so good and . . .

She barely knew what she was doing, but a need filled her mind, and a greedy desire muddled her senses. She sniffed at the wood again, and the whole world seemed to melt away. Vila's *kokoshnik*, Torniv, her father, even Koschei the Deathless — they all disappeared when faced with this new desire. She opened her mouth and brought the wood to her lips.

CHAPTER 15

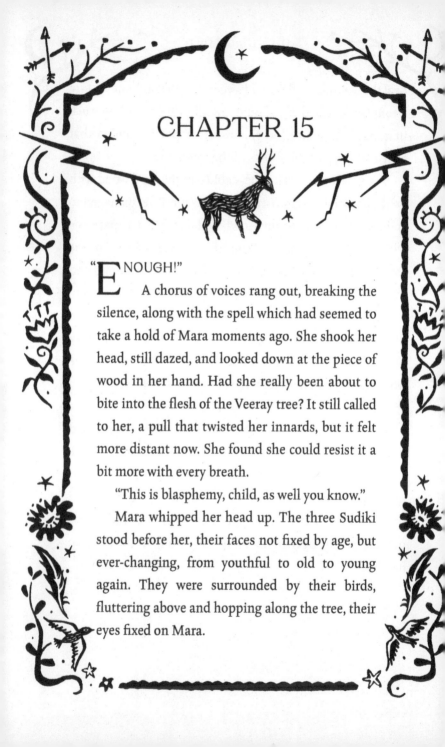

"ENOUGH!"

A chorus of voices rang out, breaking the silence, along with the spell which had seemed to take a hold of Mara moments ago. She shook her head, still dazed, and looked down at the piece of wood in her hand. Had she really been about to bite into the flesh of the Veeray tree? It still called to her, a pull that twisted her innards, but it felt more distant now. She found she could resist it a bit more with every breath.

"This is blasphemy, child, as well you know."

Mara whipped her head up. The three Sudiki stood before her, their faces not fixed by age, but ever-changing, from youthful to old to young again. They were surrounded by their birds, fluttering above and hopping along the tree, their eyes fixed on Mara.

"It's good to see you again, Aunties," Mara said, after clearing her throat. She added as much bluster to her words as she was able. With gods, it was always important to strike the right note, even if your vision was still blurry and your tongue felt like a dry lump of clay in your mouth.

One of the three sisters stepped forward. "We didn't invite you, Mara. You are not welcome."

The second sister lay a hand on the first one's shoulder. "You were our guest before, Mara. Now you're an intruder. An unexpected one."

The third sister threw her rapidly greying hair over her shoulder with a huff. "And if the fates do not expect you, then it follows that you have defied what we've ordained. You must leave, now."

Mara straightened herself up to her full height. The Sudiki loomed over her, but she met their gaze steadily.

The first Sudiki seemed to hesitate. "You must go, my sister is right. There are things that are, and things that must not be, and this *must not be*."

"Why are you arguing with her, sisters?" the third Sudiki asked. "Child, give us the wood you've stolen and leave, now."

Mara raised an eyebrow and smiled. The fates were used to people following their wishes. She just had to see what would happen if she didn't.

"I'll give you the wood if you give me Vila's *kokoshnik*."

The Sudiki took a collective breath, and the birds at their feet squawked in outrage, rising up like a cloud.

"You're not in a position to dictate the terms, granddaughter of Stribog," the second sister said. Her white, unseeing eyes turned darker and clearer until they were, once more, bright with youth and anger. "The splinter you took does not belong to you!"

Mara laughed, though the wood in her hand felt hot and sharp. She hoped the slick feeling in her palm was sweat, and not blood. "I bet Vila would say *her kokoshnik* doesn't belong to *you*! Give it back and I'll give you the wood."

The third Sudiki raised an arm and a particularly vicious-looking bird, with wings the colour of soured milk and red-rimmed black eyes, fluttered down and perched on her wrist. She glanced at Mara, stroking the bird's head. "It's not a negotiation, wind child. At any moment, we can order our birds to attack you. And how will you go back to look for your human friends if your eyes are pecked out?"

"How will you walk if the flesh is ripped off your legs?"

"How will you talk if your tongue is pulled out?"

Mara tensed, but she didn't move. You don't run from a predator. And you don't show fear in front of the gods. "What if I turn to a snowy blizzard and freeze your precious birds? Who will carry the Root Souls back to the earth then?" She gritted her teeth. The wood in her hand seemed to move of its own accord, sawing slowly through the skin and the muscle, pulsating with the same life as the branches under her feet.

The first Sudiki laughed, throwing her head back. Mara winced to see the gleaming white teeth pushing through the goddess's pale gums. "What you lack in powers, you make up for in hubris, little Mara! Don't you think the fates know that you are powerless?" She narrowed her eyes and smiled unpleasantly. "You have both your fate and your death written on your face, granddaughter of Stribog. And Koschei's name is etched into your skin, though you can't see it. He will kill you and your name will be forgotten. That is your destiny, and we should know. We have written it." The goddess laughed again, and this time her sisters joined her. Even their birds hopped around excitedly.

Mara chewed on the inside of her cheek till she tasted blood. She would not budge and she would not flinch.

"But before you die, and die you will, you will give us back what you stole, little halfling," the second Sudiki said. She took a step forward, her eyes fixed on Mara's hand. "Look, child, the tree longs to become whole again. The blood from your thieving hand is pooling at your feet. Give it back and be gone!"

Mara risked a glance down. Blood was indeed dripping from her tightened fist, but this meant nothing. It didn't mean the Sudiki were right. She raised her head and saw the three sisters creeping towards her, their eyes feverish with greed and need.

"Give me the *kokoshnik* and I will give you the wood," she said again. Her head spun and she felt like she was going to throw up.

"I don't think so,' the first Sudiki said. "The *kokoshnik* was given to us. To keep, and keep safe. It brings a balance to the world, with the Goddess of Lightning no longer rising to the sky as she wills."

The third sister nodded. "We write out the fate of every creature alive, Mara. And the gods and goddesses of chaos must not be allowed to rewrite it as the mood strikes them. Vila must not fly free again, unless we will it. Veles understands this."

"Veles is using your pride to get himself a very useful servant!" Mara put her hand to her forehead. She was sweating, and it was hard to stay upright. "You think you're writing fate and making all the rules, and to make sure of that you made a deal with the actual trickster god – and, surprise, surprise he *tricked* you!"

The three Sudiki sisters froze. The third one, who was beginning to get on Mara's nerves, put her hand on her hip and sneered. "You're a child. You can't begin to know the ways of gods. Veles is an ally, and you're a blip, a blight, a speck of dust we must brush off our shoulders, after which you will be forgotten."

"I'm the speck of dust who tricked your *ally* and stole Alatnir. I'm the blight who now has a piece of your precious Veeray tree in my hand!" Mara gritted her teeth. "So believe me, I know what I'm talking about when I say you're being used."

"Can it be, sisters?" The first Sudiki turned to the other two, uncertain.

"But we are the ones who have the golden *kokoshnik*," the second sister said. She nervously pulled on her rapidly thinning hair and didn't seem to notice the strands which had fallen out and were piling at her feet. Mara nearly gagged.

"And he's the one with the powerful servant," Mara said.

The three Sudiki looked at each other.

"Can it be?"

"The child is tricking us!"

"Then why is Vila the servant of Veles, and not us?"

There was a silence after that.

"Give me the *kokoshnik*," Mara said. "Vila is a goddess for a reason. You say she's chaos. I say she brings balance. You're the order of the universe. You're telling me you can't handle a bit of lightning?"

The sisters seemed to hesitate.

"It will teach Veles for using you," Mara added, hopefully.

The third sister narrowed her eyes. "Give us the splinter of wood. Then we'll *consider* giving you the *kokoshnik*."

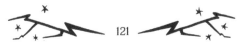

121

"Give me the *kokoshnik* and I'll give you the splinter."

"It's killing you, wind child," the second Sudiki said. "There's blood dripping from your hand. You can barely stand. It's draining you. The tree of life must be complete. It longs for the energy your body can't provide."

"Don't worry about me," Mara said, leaning against a branch in what she hoped looked like a nonchalant pose.

"Maybe we'll just wait for you to die, and then pick the splinter from the dried-up husk of your hand?"

Mara knew they were right. She could barely stand. She held up the splinter in front of her face so she could see it. Then she opened her mouth.

"Don't!"

"Blasphemy!"

The sisters clasped hands and above them rose the cloud of their birds.

"It will kill you, you know!"

"Sounds like a lot of things are killing me or looking to kill me or planning to kill me or, if I understand you right, *will* inevitably kill me, so why shouldn't I chance doing something you clearly don't want me to do?"

The third Sudiki laughed. "You are truly Stribog's granddaughter."

"I'm my father's daughter," Mara said. She was getting tired of 'wind child this' and 'wind child that'. "For the fates, you don't seem to understand humans all that much."

"Oh, but we understand *you*, little one." The first Sudiki stepped forward. Mara moved her hand closer to her mouth in warning and the goddess stilled. "You were your father's daughter once, that's true. We saw your brown hair and eyes, your pale human skin, when you first came to us. But that spark of mortality is gone. Your human soul is gone, and only the storm remains."

"Oh, but look, sister!" the second sister said. "Her eyes flit about. She doesn't believe us. She thinks she can trick her way back to humanity. A river which hopes to flow back out of the sea."

Mara winced. The second sister giggled like a mean-spirited child.

"You *did* think that, didn't you? That, after you're free of Koschei, you'll be able to lie and cheat and steal your soul back from Veles? It's no longer there, Mara." The goddess turned her head to the side, watching Mara with curiosity. "Your mortal soul has long since flown up into the Milky Way to rest among the stars. What's left is all that's left and all that will be. Incomplete, a chipped cup. Not worth fighting for."

Mara's hand dropped to her side. She fought back the tears threatening to fill her eyes. She shook her head. "I don't believe you. And even if I did, I'll find the way. And even if I don't, even if I'm not worth saving, Torniv is. His brother is. And, to save them, I need the *kokoshnik*!"

The three goddess sisters stood silent for a moment.

"Very well," the first sister said. "You have bought yourself a chance, Mara. But that's all. One chance."

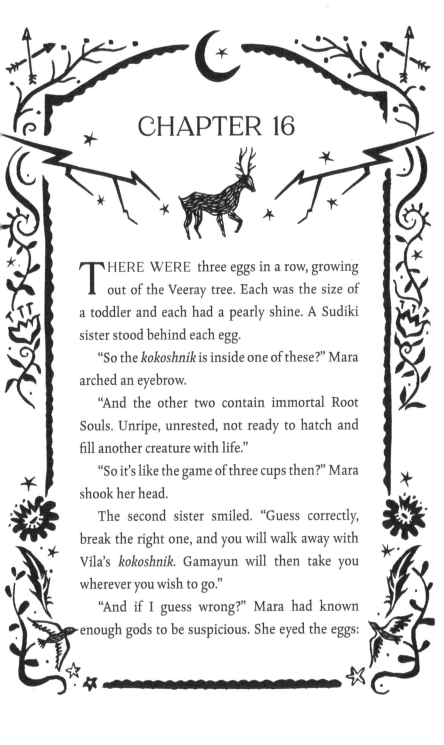

CHAPTER 16

THERE WERE three eggs in a row, growing out of the Veeray tree. Each was the size of a toddler and each had a pearly shine. A Sudiki sister stood behind each egg.

"So the *kokoshnik* is inside one of these?" Mara arched an eyebrow.

"And the other two contain immortal Root Souls. Unripe, unrested, not ready to hatch and fill another creature with life."

"So it's like the game of three cups then?" Mara shook her head.

The second sister smiled. "Guess correctly, break the right one, and you will walk away with Vila's *kokoshnik*. Gamayun will then take you wherever you wish to go."

"And if I guess wrong?" Mara had known enough gods to be suspicious. She eyed the eggs:

perfect, shiny and smooth. She didn't want to meet a bird capable of laying an egg that size, that's for sure.

"If you break an egg with a Root Soul inside, its unformed essence will fly into the air and disappear, never to be reborn again. It will never breathe or live among the mortals."

"And you'd be ok with that?" Mara scratched the back of her head. "With me just destroying one of the souls it's your job to protect?"

"We'd still get a soul in the end in either case, Stribog's granddaughter." The Sudiki sister who spoke smiled toothlessly. "The balance will always be preserved. The Veeray tree will make sure of it."

"By taking one of my two remaining souls, I would imagine?" Mara tried to sound composed but swallowed hard. She shuddered, remembering the moment her human soul had been peeled off her. The sickening ripping noise as she felt layers of herself being separated and pulled apart. "Would I even survive that?"

"Of course not."

Well, that's refreshing honesty. Mara managed a crooked smile and approached the eggs.

"Aren't you forgetting something?" One of the Sudiki held out her palm.

"You want the one shred of security I have in this place for the privilege of giving me a chance to kill myself?" Mara held out the piece of wood between her thumb and forefinger. "What guarantee do I have you will let me leave with the *kokoshnik* if I guess right?"

"We are the Sudiki," one of the sisters smiled a little too knowingly. "If it's your destiny to pass this test, then we wouldn't dream of interfering. We are the fates. We're just the humble servants of the paths of time."

Mara rolled her eyes. *Humble, my foot.* She held out the splinter and dropped it into the goddess's hand. "It's a deal, Auntie." The moment she dropped the sliver of wood into the Sudiki's hand she felt as if a boulder had been lifted off her back. She blinked a few times. She needed to shake this off, this fog clouding her judgement. She'd get one chance to guess right. There could be no mistakes. Torniv's life depended on it, as well as her own.

She walked nearer to the eggs. Up close, she could see they were not identical at all. Their colours were slightly different and she could see a pattern on each, as faint as the cloud of a baby's breath in Winter. *As different as the souls inside.*

She placed her hand on each egg in turn. They were not as smooth as she had expected. The surface of their shells felt porous under her fingertips. They all felt warm and dry.

She inspected the way the eggs were attached to the tree, each growing from a nest-like indentation in the bark.

Nothing to help her choose.

She sat on her bottom and stared at the eggs in frustration.

There was no hint, no symbols she could decipher, nothing!

She folded her arms on her knees and rested her chin on them.

"Choose well, Mara," a familiar voice whispered. Gamayun stood in front of the eggs, hopping from one leg to the other on great talons. Mara nodded a greeting.

The Sudiki stood aside, watching her carefully. Mara cast a furtive glance at the goddesses. They tried to keep their faces still, at least as still as their constantly changing features would allow. Mara frowned. The three sisters' bodies were tense, with the forced nonchalance of bad card players.

Mara turned to the three eggs again. *What did Mama Bohyna say?* 'The audience sees what they want and the trick is to keep them looking in the wrong direction'.

"I choose none of them," Mara said.

She laughed at the collective gasp from the three sisters.

The third sister shushed the others and said, "Do you give up then?"

"That's not what I said, and you know it." Mara stood up and faced the Sudiki.

"If you forfeit your chance to guess then—"

"Again, that's not what I said." Mara smiled. "All three eggs have Root Souls in them. None of them have the *kokoshnik*. I solved the puzzle, I won. Hand over Vila's headdress."

"The test was to break one of the eggs," one of the Sudiki protested.

"The deal was to guess which of the eggs contained the *kokoshnik*. I guessed right. The rest is just you trying to kill me, Auntie. And a lot of folk have been trying to kill me for a long while now. I know the look."

"You have made a promise, Sudiki." Gamayun's voice echoed through the air. She stretched her magnificent wings. "It was witnessed by myself and the Veeray tree itself. The course is set. You must honour the agreement you made with Stribog's granddaughter."

The three sisters looked at one another. Something in the air seemed to shift as a thread of understanding passed between them. The Sudiki all raised their arms in the air, and a light almost too bright to bear shone across the many woven branches of the Veeray tree. Then, in front of the three goddesses lay the most beautiful headdress Mara had ever seen, and she'd seen plenty of her mother's ornaments. Vila's *kokoshnik* was a half-circle, like the setting sun, golden but for the ruby thread running through it like a crack of lightning in the sky.

Mara picked it up. It was surprisingly light. A spark came off it the moment Mara's fingers touched the surface, which raised the small hairs on her forearms.

"We have kept to our agreement, wind child," the Sudiki said in unison.

Mara turned her attention to them.

"We have given you the *kokoshnik*." The third Sudiki

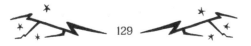

129

sister narrowed her eyes. "But letting you leave with it wasn't a part of the deal."

The three goddesses clasped hands and their swarm of birds began circling above Mara's head like locusts.

Mara swore under her breath. Her hand fished inside the pocket of her skirt and she threw one of Mama Bohyna's clay bombs as far as she could towards the Sudiki. She dropped to the ground and covered her head just as the bomb exploded, the pale purple smoke obscuring everything in sight. The Sudiki screamed in outrage, as their birds flew to shield them.

The sound of flapping wings above her told Mara clearly that Mama Bohyna's gift had only given her a moment, a thought's-worth of a pause, before the cloud dispersed and the remaining birds descended upon her.

Mara looked at the *kokoshnik* in her hands. If everyone wanted it, then surely it must have been used for something besides looking pretty.

The birds let out a screech and formed an arrow, getting closer and closer. Mara closed her eyes and put the *kokoshnik* on her head.

A flash of lightning pierced the sky. A smell of singed feathers hit Mara's nostrils. *And I thought the one eagle-feather candle smelled bad!*

She opened her eyes. Feathers were falling around her, with the unhit birds flying away in all directions. Mara's ears were ringing from the noise. The Sudiki were wailing in the distance.

She looked at her hands. Had she just commanded lightning?

"I'll have it back now, wind child," a voice rang before her.

Mara snapped her head up. There, hovering just a few steps away, was Vila, her face flushed and eyes sparkling.

Oh. Mara looked at her hands. Of course it hadn't been her own powers. She took the golden headdress off and handed it over to the Goddess of Lightning.

Vila placed it on her head. "And my ring?"

"I know where it is," Mara said. "But I don't know how to get there."

Vila smiled. "Maybe I can help."

Mara waved at Gamayun, who smiled and nodded a goodbye.

Vila picked up Mara and carried her away from the Veeray tree.

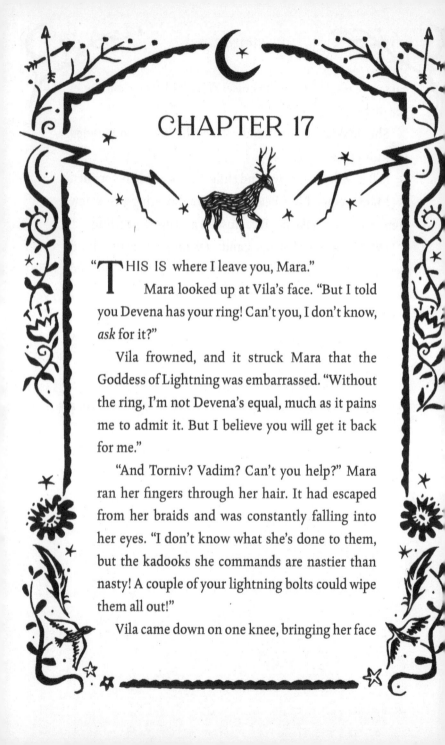

CHAPTER 17

"THIS IS where I leave you, Mara."

Mara looked up at Vila's face. "But I told you Devena has your ring! Can't you, I don't know, *ask* for it?"

Vila frowned, and it struck Mara that the Goddess of Lightning was embarrassed. "Without the ring, I'm not Devena's equal, much as it pains me to admit it. But I believe you will get it back for me."

"And Torniv? Vadim? Can't you help?" Mara ran her fingers through her hair. It had escaped from her braids and was constantly falling into her eyes. "I don't know what she's done to them, but the kadooks she commands are nastier than nasty! A couple of your lightning bolts could wipe them all out!"

Vila came down on one knee, bringing her face

closer to Mara's. "There are rules out there, little Mara, which must be obeyed, even by the gods. Without my ring, I'm not my own master. But if you get it for me, I will help you face your enemy."

Mara shrugged. "Very convenient, especially since I need your help right this moment."

Vila grinned and rose higher and higher till she blended in with the morning light.

"Right." Mara sat and redid her braids. Her fingers worked quickly, the rhythm soothing. Devena was the Goddess of the Hunt. The answer had to be there. Some angle Mara could work. Some weakness staring her right in the face. But right now, the answers eluded Mara and she knew she was painfully exposed. She didn't even have Vila's charm anymore. *She was such an idiot!* She groaned. Why hadn't she asked Vila for another one?

Mara held the end of her braid in front of her face. She had few allies and even fewer friends, and she would have to do what was necessary.

She used her knife to cut a strand of her hair before once more securing the end of her braid. She looked around for a few pinecones and put them in a circle, but not before digging the last single pine nut out of one of them. She sighed and placed her hair onto the pinecones.

She dropped the little white nut into the circle and took a step back. "Aunt Borova! Uncle Borovy! Please come!"

She waited for a long time. There was no answer. She tugged at her braid in frustration. She looked around the forest floor and found a shrivelled old mushroom, wormy and soggy. A less than ideal offering, but then she herself was a less than ideal petitioner. She placed the mushroom in the middle of the pinecone circle and again raised her voice. "Aunt Borova, Uncle Borovy! It's me, Mara! I need you! Please answer!"

There was nothing but the silence of the forest, which was no silence at all, with the birds and the beetles screeching and buzzing out their amusement. Mara kneeled in front of her offering. The soft damp moss was soaking her trousers, but she didn't care.

She didn't know where the kadooks had taken Torniv and Vadim. She didn't know what Devena intended for them. She hit her temples rhythmically. *Think, Mara, think!*

She could do it; she could figure it out. Uncle Borovy wouldn't answer her call? Fine. Evidently, he and his wife still bore a grudge from when she had tricked them right at the beginning of her journey. She made them offer shelter to a deer they believed was destined to die. The fact they grew to love it in the end was apparently beside the point. But that was what they did, wasn't it? Bargain and negotiate, and sometimes you came out ahead and sometimes you didn't, and right now she had nothing to negotiate with. She squeezed her eyes shut, but the tears came anyway, rolling down her cheeks and into the ground.

A soft rumble startled Mara. She scrambled away from the circle of pinecones. Was it the kadooks again? It took her a moment to realise what was happening and, when she did, a huge grin brightened her face.

The earth beneath the pinecone crown crumbled and broke apart and Aunt Borova rose up, hunched over and as small and round as ever. She opened her bead-black eyes and stared at Mara for a moment.

Mara rushed towards her with a laugh but stopped short, as there were no open arms to greet her, nor a smile on the unusually serious face.

"Thank you for coming, Aunt," Mara said.

"I could hardly help it, could I, with you crying your ice tears on my head?"

Mara bit her lip and hurriedly wiped her face with her sleeve. She realised she'd never seen Aunt Borova's face without a smile. Without its usual amused expression, Aunt Borova's face seemed even less human, its long sharp nose and small eyes making her appear almost insect-like.

"I see you've shed your humanity as easily as the mountains shake off the snow in the Spring," Aunt Borova scoffed and moved her hand as if trying to wave away a bad smell. "You shouldn't be here."

Calmly does it. "You seem unhappy, Aunt, though it's been a while since you last saw me."

Aunt Borova's mouth twisted in a mocking smile. "Yes, and it would have been the last time if you'd had any sense. I can sense my husband on the wind, child, and you better say your piece now. We want no part of your current troubles."

"What do you know of my troubles?" Mara's eyebrows shot up.

"Far too much, child of the winds!" Uncle Borovy strode into the clearing, his legs creaking like dry pines in the storm. He was, as ever, surrounded by his animals, the wolves and the birds of prey ever circling above his head. "For your troubles are like the plague, spreading on the wind to all those foolish enough to be near you. I will make no more bargains with you!" Uncle Borovy's eyes swirled angrily, the red-hot amber of them fixed on Mara, who was smart enough not to look directly into them. Uncle Borovy was known to blind those who displeased him, and she was clearly not in his good graces that day.

Mara looked behind him instead, at a beautiful white deer, its wide eyes meeting Mara's with the familiarity of old friends.

"Sniezinka!" Mara's face brightened, as if the Guardian of the Forest wasn't towering over her, his wolves baring their fangs and his falcons circling above her, ready to pick her bones clean. "I'm so glad to see her grown and healthy!"

Uncle Borovy's features softened with affection as he glanced towards the deer. "Did you doubt she would be?

When I gave my promise I'd watch over her?"

Mara smiled up at him. "Just as I promised you she'd be your pride and joy, and so she has become. It seems to *me* that one could even say you benefit from our bargains, at least as much as I do."

"Don't try to charm us, child. We know of the curse on you, and of who hunts you," Aunt Borova cut in, clearly displeased with her husband's calmer expression. "You must leave our forest, lest you bring the Deathless one's attention to it. We can protect the forest from pestilence and fire and even the greed of men, but we can't protect it from Koschei should he turn his sights on us!" Aunt Borova looked up as if she expected Koschei to appear before them, then and there.

Uncle Borovy faced Mara, the anger in his eyes turning to something like . . . *pity*. Mara winced at the thought. "We also know the Goddess of the Hunt is after you. I feel her monstrosities tearing up the ground of my forest, rendering the roots of my beautiful trees apart. They're hunting for you, child. The sooner you leave, the sooner we will be left alone."

"She has Torniv," Mara said. "She has Torniv's brother. And one other thing that doesn't belong to her."

Uncle Borovy laughed, though his wife held on to the anger still marking her face. "And you plan to take it from her? You hear that, wife?"

Aunt Borova sniffed and turned her face away, though it

held a troubled expression. "Let her at it then. The Goddess of the Hunt will hunt her, and tear the foolish child to shreds, and that, at least, will be the end to our troubles."

"They're my friends. I do not abandon my friends. You were a friend to me once, Aunt." She let the accusation sit there between them.

Aunt Borova stared at Mara for a while. "Our responsibility is not to you, child." Her voice seemed to have softened, though the words were hard. "We guard the forest, but we cannot fulfil our obligations while Devena is here. The hunt is on, my child. Not of the natural sort, either." She closed her eyes, her lash-less eyelids a shade darker than the skin of her cheeks. "The eagle hunts the rabbit, the lynx hunts the deer, and the balance of the forest is kept. Devena hunts for the joy of it, not to satisfy a need. And the animals and men around her lose the sight of what, or *who,* they're after, and all they feel is the thirst and a desire for the blood to stain their faces."

Uncle Borovy swayed like a tall pine before coming down to a crouch, his joints creaking. He lifted Mara's chin with a four-jointed finger. "Men worship her not for who she is, but who they wish she was. She calls herself the 'Goddess of the Hunt', wind child, but she's the goddess of blood lust. A sister of lightning and one of the two Goddesses of Chaos. She twists those around her until all they can hear and see is their prey and the triumph of the kill. Your friend, Torniv, is not how you left him. You cannot save him now, child."

"What do you mean?" A chill ran down Mara's spine, her light-blue skin turning paler. "What did she do?"

"Mara, she turned the boy, Vadim, into a golden stag," Aunt Borova said. "And Torniv-the-bear is hunting his brother."

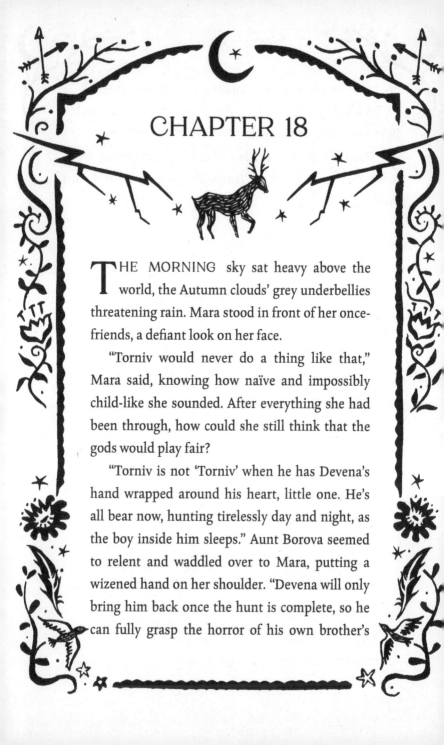

CHAPTER 18

THE MORNING sky sat heavy above the world, the Autumn clouds' grey underbellies threatening rain. Mara stood in front of her once-friends, a defiant look on her face.

"Torniv would never do a thing like that," Mara said, knowing how naïve and impossibly child-like she sounded. After everything she had been through, how could she still think that the gods would play fair?

"Torniv is not 'Torniv' when he has Devena's hand wrapped around his heart, little one. He's all bear now, hunting tirelessly day and night, as the boy inside him sleeps." Aunt Borova seemed to relent and waddled over to Mara, putting a wizened hand on her shoulder. "Devena will only bring him back once the hunt is complete, so he can fully grasp the horror of his own brother's blood on his hands. And unless you leave, you will condemn him to be *your* executioner as well. Leave, child. Live. There is nothing you can do here."

Mara stood very still for a moment. There was a defiant look on her face, even though she felt the weight of the world weighing her down.

"You can help me," Mara said. "Let me ride Sniezinka. She's strong and grown and will allow me to evade Torniv, so I can find a way to free him."

"No." Uncle Borovy's moss-covered eyebrows knitted together. "Our first deal was done. I don't owe you a mount anymore, and I will not let my favourite deer die with you."

"Tell me what you want in exchange for this favour, Uncle." Mara stood tall, her legs wide, her arms crossed on her chest. "There's always a bargain to be struck. Always a negotiation. And I'm not even haggling. Name your price for your help, and I will pay it. Tell me what you want of mine, and I will give it. I might be the least of Stribog's grandchildren, but I'm still his, and I have worth."

"Bold words," Aunt Borova said. She raised a hand to silence the protest from her husband. She walked around Mara, like a farmer inspecting a yearling cow at the market. She lifted Mara's braid with her walking stick, and then let it fall.

"Your hair is now like your mother's," she noticed. "The loss of your human soul is our gain. I will have your hair."

"You want my braid?" Mara said. "But what can you possibly want it for? You already have some of my mother's hair."

"Not your braid, silly child," Aunt Borova guffawed, glancing towards her unamused husband. "*All* of your hair. You ask much of us. I will have all you can give in return." She took in Mara's shocked expression. "Never you mind what I want it for, but I do want it, and I will have it."

Mara nodded.

"Now," Aunt Borova continued walking around Mara, "we will give you one thing, and one thing only. We will let you ride Sniezinka, if she'll have you, of course."

Mara glanced towards the deer. The animal walked up to her and made a small bow. Mara placed her hand on Sniezinka's forehead and nodded. "Thank you," she said.

"Take care no harm should befall her." Aunt Borova lifted a finger. "Don't incur debts you cannot pay." There was a threat in the words.

"Do you accept?" Aunt Borova asked.

Mara kneeled in front of her, her face down.

Aunt Borova clasped Mara's face in both hands, and moved her fingers up as if she was running them through Mara's hair. A soft sensation made Mara look down, as a lock of hair fell onto her knees.

The forest guardian's nails moved soundlessly, shearing the hair off Mara's head. The twin braids fell to the ground with a muffled thud. Mara closed her eyes, not wishing to see it. It was just hair, just hair, just nothing. A tear rolled down her cheek.

At long last, Aunt Borova was finished. She picked up the hair with care, placing it inside her pocket. "Very well," she said, her voice softer. "It's done."

Mara's hand rose to her scalp, which suddenly felt much colder. She shook her head and forced a smile. "Feels much lighter." She felt naked. If only she still had Vadim's hat.

The white doe approached and nudged Mara's shoulder with her nose.

"Do you think she remembers me?" Mara said to Uncle Borovy, scratching the animal behind the ear.

"Of course," Uncle Borovy smiled, the hard bark-like skin of his face cracking with the effort. "She's one of mine. We don't forget our debts. Go now, Mara." He sniffed at the air.

Aunt Borova ran her finger across Mara's cheek in a caress. "The hunt is on."

CHAPTER 19

SNIEZINKA GALLOPED across the forest, twisting and turning to avoid the trees. Mara clung to her back, making herself small, as the tree branches and bushes scratched at her sides. A roar echoed across the canopy.

"We are close," Mara whispered, holding on tight to the animal's neck. "Keep downwind of him. Torniv can smell a mouse in its burrow. I don't want him to smell us."

There were no birds singing above their heads. *Uncle Borovy must be keeping them hidden and safe*, thought Mara. It made the rhythmical thud of Sniezinka's hooves all the more unnerving.

Mara's ears were ringing with the drum of her heart: so loud; so terribly, terribly loud. *They must be deaf to not hear it*, she thought, and a shiver ran down her spine. She was sure that Devena must have sensed her presence, that even now the kadooks were slithering beneath the ground, waiting for the chance to snap Sniezinka's legs and pull Mara to the ground.

But it would do no one any good for Mara to allow this madness to take over. She had to save Vadim. Because if she failed, there would be no saving Torniv.

She knew the exact moment when she came into the aura of Devena.

A hunger rumbled through her belly, and her heart started beating with a fury she didn't know or recognise. She bit her lip, until blood ran down her chin. There was an anger burrowing its way into her heart.

Above her rose a noise, unnatural in its intensity. Those among the forest's creatures unlucky enough to have evaded Uncle Borovy's protection were filled with the same hunger as Mara. A battle raged above, the tangled branches of the woods bearing witness. Feathers fell in a flurry. Sparrows and finches flew into each other: chasing, ripping, tearing, pecking. Speckles of their blood dripped onto the moss and onto Sniezinka's white coat.

Mara shut her eyes tight, trusting in her mount. If she let in the hunger and the anger, she'd be lost. She had to think of something else, anything else, anything strong enough to push Devena out. So she thought of peace; of music; of her grandmother, Sorona, sitting by the fireplace. A pang of sadness hit her right in the chest. She'd kept it at bay, all this time. But if she let herself feel sad now, then she would stop noticing the way Sniezinka's neck strained, the muscles and the tendons of it, the warmth of the skin under Mara's fingertips . . .

Mara let herself feel the sadness and the loss. Her human soul was gone. Her da was gone. Her mother, her home, her future . . .

A sob shook her shoulders. Tears were streaming down her face. She felt like the pain would crush the life out of her.

And then, the hunger was gone. She'd pushed it out. She could still feel Devena's influence, but she'd pushed it out. A small victory. The smallest of the victories she had to win if she was going to survive what was to come.

The wind changed, and Sniezinka turned. The roar was behind them now.

"Sniezinka, can you find Vadim?" Mara whispered, feeling uncertain. "He's turned to a stag, but he's not one really." Mara sighed. Was it foolish to talk to the deer? She was just an animal after all, no different from the others, except for her proximity to the gods. But Sniezinka changed direction and, in what seemed like a few heartbeats later, a reddish gold blur appeared between the trees. *There you are.* Mara grinned.

"Run alongside him," she asked, and soon she was beside Vadim. A short sharp scream escaped him, followed by a grunt. One large dark-brown eye swivelled in its socket,

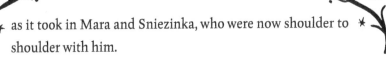

as it took in Mara and Sniezinka, who were now shoulder to shoulder with him.

"It's me, Mara!" Mara called out.

He made no sign of hearing her.

A roar sounded behind them. Mara risked turning her head, holding tight to Sniezinka's neck.

A monster bounded out of the forest. Even though the bear behind them looked like Torniv in his transformed state, there was no recognition in his eyes. He roared in excitement. *The thrill of an imminent kill . . .*

Mara shuddered, her whole body glued to her mount's back. Nothing had ever scared her this much. Not Lubac the Serpent, not Baba Latingorka, nor any of the horrors in her cave. One look at Torniv and she knew, without a shadow of a doubt, that her friend would kill her if she let him. He would tear her throat out without hesitation.

Devena did this to him.

A kernel of anger grew within Mara's chest, but it wasn't the aimless, blinding fury of the goddess's making. This was a clear purpose, a determination so sharp-edged, it could cut glass.

"To the side," Mara leaned forward and whispered in Sniezinka's ear. The deer seemed to understand. It sped up, turning away from Vadim, and into the thicket, bounding over the fallen logs.

The bear followed Mara and Sniezinka, allowing Vadim

to turn the other way. A simple trick, but Torniv would be back on his brother's trail soon enough if no slower prey could be caught first.

Torniv was fast, but he lacked the deer's agility. Soon, Mara could no longer see or hear him behind them, though she knew well enough he was there, sniffing the air, dead-eyed and hungry beyond the needs of his body.

"Viatroduya!" Mara looked up and screamed into the air. The air seemed still, but Viatroduya would be there. The most vicious of the vicious wind spirits, he was always there. Always listening, always eavesdropping, always spying.

A chilling cold ran across her scalp and a peal of laughter sounded in the distance, bouncing off the trees in an endless echo.

"I know you hear me! Come to me!"

A sudden gust of air, appearing from nowhere, blew dirt into Mara's face and Sniezinka's eyes. The deer grunted in shock and bucked, nearly throwing Mara off her back.

You dare speak to me like this, little halfling? Little nothing. An unripe berry, a pretender with your blue skin, like you belong to Stribog, like you matter? A vicious whisper made Mara rub her ear with irritation.

"Half-nothing, Viatroduya! Haven't you heard? I'm all god blood now!" Mara smiled to herself.

Then what need have you of me, if you're so swollen with the power of Stribog's blood? The voice was mocking, but then

Viatroduya mocked everybody. There was no new attack, no more sand in her eyes. That was a good sign.

"My powers are not of that sort, Viatroduya! The changing wind is your speciality!"

And why should I help you, when it would be so much easier and so much more delicious to watch your friend tear you to shreds?

A grunt from Sniezinka made Mara realise she'd been digging her nails into the animal's skin. "Sorry," she whispered.

"As much fun as watching me die would be for you, you might not enjoy my grandfather's fury, which he would rain upon you for that small pleasure."

There was a silence after that. Viatroduya's voice came through smaller, quieter, as he considered Mara's words.

Stribog could help you himself if he wanted to. He's not here and so he doesn't wish to help you . . . so he wouldn't be cross with his servant for doing the same.

"Have you *met* my grandfather?" Mara laughed. "He might not help me himself, but to find his *servant* . . ." she paused on the word, "his *servant* had dared to refuse a request by his own granddaughter . . . That would not go down well with him. He might not punish you for the deed today or tomorrow. But then the wind will change, as it always does. And he will tear you up till you are nothing but the whistle of the wind."

A long pause followed, during which Mara could hear nothing but her own blood rushing in her ears and the steady rhythm of Sniezinka's hooves beating the ground. It would do no good to hurry this. She had to let Viatroduya *imagine* her grandfather's fury. She had to let it sink in.

What do you want? The question hung in the air like an accusation.

"I need you to change the direction of the wind. Keep it away from us. Keep it so that me and Sniezinka, *and* Vadim the stag, are downwind of Torniv at all times. Confuse him. Carry our scent so he thinks we're ahead of him when we're behind. Keep us hidden: the noise of the hooves, the smell of our sweat, *all* of it. Make us invisible, Viatroduya. Unless you can't do it . . ." She allowed herself a smile. She didn't doubt he'd find a way to pay her back for it later.

Viatroduya didn't reply at first, but then came a promise: *Never call me again, Mara Gontovna. I will never again come to your aid after today.*

Mara felt a shift in the air, a change to the natural pattern of the wind.

"Turn right, Sniezinka," Mara said. "We're the hunters now."

CHAPTER 20

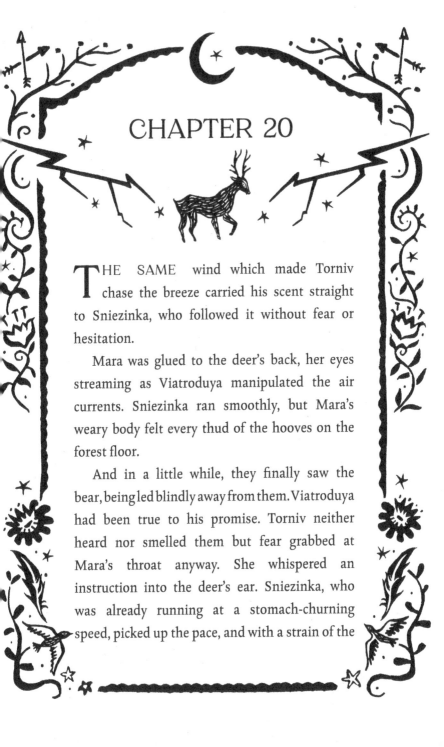

THE SAME wind which made Torniv chase the breeze carried his scent straight to Sniezinka, who followed it without fear or hesitation.

Mara was glued to the deer's back, her eyes streaming as Viatroduya manipulated the air currents. Sniezinka ran smoothly, but Mara's weary body felt every thud of the hooves on the forest floor.

And in a little while, they finally saw the bear, being led blindly away from them. Viatroduya had been true to his promise. Torniv neither heard nor smelled them but fear grabbed at Mara's throat anyway. She whispered an instruction into the deer's ear. Sniezinka, who was already running at a stomach-churning speed, picked up the pace, and with a strain of the powerful hind legs, she ran to Torniv's side and leapt above him.

There was no time for a breath as Mara let go of the deer's neck and tumbled on top of what was once her friend. She grabbed huge handfuls of his fur and kicked with her legs as her body was dragged this way and that.

Torniv roared and turned around, snapping his jaws furiously, trying to grab Mara's body as she scrambled to climb on top of him.

Within a moment too short for a prayer, Mara's foot had found a solid bit of a tree root and she pushed against it, hauling herself on top of Torniv. A low growl escaped his throat.

"It's me, Mara!" Mara screamed as Torniv tried to shake her off. "You're not this! Fight it, Torniv!" But Torniv either couldn't hear her or he didn't understand, because there was nothing human in his roar, as he staggered between the trees, bumping against their trunks to try and knock Mara to the ground. She kept her legs curled up tight underneath her to stop them from getting crushed.

Torniv soon realised he wasn't getting her off that way, so he fell to the ground, crushing her under his tremendous weight, snapping his maws as he twisted this way and that. Mara heard the cracking of her ribs as her body flooded with pain. Still, she held on.

Torniv stood up again and shook his back. Mara gritted

her teeth and, risking a second with a lopsided hold, reached into her pocket and pulled out Mama Bohyna's ball of clay. It felt pleasantly cool under her fingers as she pulled her arm back and flung it, as hard as she could, against the tree nearest to them.

The sound bomb filled the forest with an unearthly, piercing noise. It exploded in a series of loud whistles and crackles, and there were red sparks flying. Mara lowered her head between her shoulders as if she could block out the noise.

Torniv whimpered, his dark eyes swivelling with terror as he searched for the source of the threat. Then the fear took over.

He bounded through the forest at full speed, heedless of the low dry branches scratching his sides.

Mara clung to his back, barely daring to raise her head above the hump of his shoulders. She sucked in the air in quick, shallow breaths, as her ribs screamed in pain.

She flexed her fingers, grabbing as much of Torniv's fur as she could fit in her fists, then judged the right moment and pulled on Torniv, steering him into a sharp turn.

Torniv, too frightened and confused to see what was happening, saw the trunk of an oak too late, as his head collided with it at full speed.

Mara was thrown off Torniv's back in a half somersault, hitting the tree with her entire back. She slid down headfirst into the moss. Breathing was painful.

A flash of light lit up the outline of the small veins in Mara's closed eyelids.

"You don't know when to die, wind child."

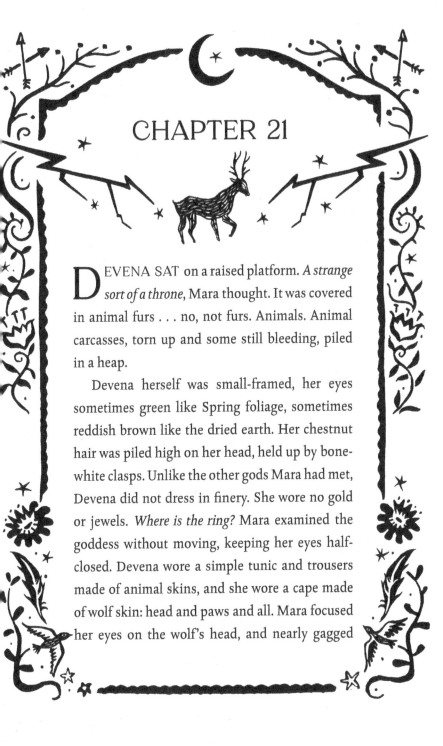

CHAPTER 21

DEVENA SAT on a raised platform. *A strange sort of a throne*, Mara thought. It was covered in animal furs . . . no, not furs. Animals. Animal carcasses, torn up and some still bleeding, piled in a heap.

Devena herself was small-framed, her eyes sometimes green like Spring foliage, sometimes reddish brown like the dried earth. Her chestnut hair was piled high on her head, held up by bone-white clasps. Unlike the other gods Mara had met, Devena did not dress in finery. She wore no gold or jewels. *Where is the ring?* Mara examined the goddess without moving, keeping her eyes half-closed. Devena wore a simple tunic and trousers made of animal skins, and she wore a cape made of wolf skin: head and paws and all. Mara focused her eyes on the wolf's head, and nearly gagged as she saw the eye move in its socket. Alert, *alive*. The wolf whose skin Devena wore was still alive, animated by the whim of the goddess.

"I know you're awake, Mara." Devena tapped her knee with her forefinger. She seemed impatient, jittery almost. Like a moment of stillness was a moment too long. Mara noted that little fact.

"Good day, goddess," Mara said. She winced. It hurt to talk, though she didn't expect Devena to care. "You seem to be displeased with me and my friends."

Devena laughed softly and rested her chin against her hand. She was leaning against, from what Mara could tell, a hare torn in half, its entrails hanging off the side of the makeshift throne.

"You're a very polite little thief, aren't you?" The goddess smiled. She seemed almost childlike, with her small pointed chin and her large eyes. A nasty, cruel little child, laughing at a fly whose wings she was about to rip out.

"A thief?" Mara raised her eyebrows. "I'm afraid I don't understand. I was travelling with my friends when we were attacked by your servants. You have nothing I want." Her eyes flitted across the goddess. *Where was that ring?*

Devena didn't disappoint. She scoffed and raised a large golden hoop, sharp-edged and the size of a stew pot's rim, which she had hooked on her belt. It was undeniably a weapon, though of a kind Mara had never seen before.

"Veles warned me you were a liar as well as a thief. You want Vila's ring, and I have little time for those seeking to rob me. You're out of luck, Stribog's kin. I'm the Goddess of the Hunt and I always, *always* strike first."

Mara composed her face into a mask of perfect innocence. "I don't want a ring. Why would I want that?"

Devena seemed confused for a moment, but then her eyebrows knitted together. "Don't lie to me, child. Your bear friend was brought to me with two of my sister's charms about him. Two charms for the two weapons Vila wants back. You have already weaseled one of them away from the Sudiki, and now you seek to trick me as well."

Mara laughed and then doubled up in pain. "You're the Goddess of the Hunt! You really think Vila would send a powerless girl and a boy to steal anything from you? Are you *my* prey now, Devena?"

Devena's eyes narrowed, the flecks of gold pooling by the narrow pupils. "I could have my kadooks rip you to shreds, little girl. Tread carefully."

Mara shivered, remembering the kadooks' blind toothy faces and pale wormy bodies. She felt as if her lungs were filled with ground glass, every breath laboured.

When a predator circles you is not the best time to show weakness, and so Mara just raised her eyebrows and smiled pleasantly. "I don't think you will, Devena. That's not the spirit of you, that's not the hunt. If Torniv . . ." she nodded towards the unconscious bear, "if Torniv had killed me, that would just be the nature of your power, just the conclusion of the hunt. But he didn't get me, and it wouldn't be very sporting to kill Stribog's granddaughter as if she was no more than a fledgling in the nest. In fact, Stribog might take issue with that."

Devena leaned back, her fingers playing with the ears of the slaughtered fox she sat on. "I'm not afraid of Stribog. And I will not let you steal what's mine. Stribog would not complain."

"Except I don't want anything of yours." Mara rolled her eyes. "Vila already has her *kokoshnik* and her ring. All I want now is to get my friends back and be on our way, without bothering you ever again."

Devena stiffened. "What are you talking about?"

"Well, you know how you turned Vadim into a stag and Torniv into a mindless monster-bear? Could you undo that, please?"

"No." Devena waved her hand impatiently. "What do you mean, 'Vila has her ring back'? Are you blind as well as stupid?" She raised the golden weapon above her head. "*This* is Vila's ring."

Mara raised one eyebrow. "If you say so. Can we go now?"

"No, you may not!" Devena stood up and strode towards Mara. The throne beneath her rotted rapidly and fell apart, the animal bodies collapsing into themselves and then falling off their bones which soon, too, fell into dust. Devena didn't seem to notice. "You will not go until I say so, and I do not say so until you explain what you mean about Vila already having her ring. There is trickery at play here and I will not be made a fool of!"

Mara sighed. "I'm not making a fool of you. In fact, I'm not making anything of you. I have neither the interest nor the time, frankly, to be playing games with one of the chaos sisters. I'm a wind spirit, Devena. Have you ever known any of us to stick our necks out unnecessarily?"

Devena crouched in front of Mara, the hood of her wolf-skin-cape exposing the long fangs in a snarl, though the goddess's face was impassive. "No, I have not, Mara. I find your kind self-serving and, all in all, rather cowardly. So I don't think any of your kin would come between me and my sister, but then I haven't known any of your kind who would put themselves in danger for the sake of two mortal children. If you're unusual in this, what's to say you're not unusual in other ways?"

"I might be unusual, but I'm not stupid," Mara said. "If I was after that trinket you call Vila's ring . . ." Mara allowed a small smile to twist her lips, ". . . I wouldn't have come so completely unprepared. I've brought no allies, no weapons. I have no magical tricks at my disposal, not even anything to barter with. Look at me." She pointed to her shorn scalp. "How would I take a weapon off a goddess like you?"

Devena seemed to consider this. Mara cast a quick glance towards Torniv. His chest was moving rhythmically. She closed her eyes for a moment, relieved the impact into the tree hadn't killed him.

"It would be stupid of you to try to steal from me." Devena lifted Mara's chin and looked into her eyes. Mara forced herself to meet the goddess's gaze. Devena's fingers were warm and rough, like a cat's tongue. "But if you say this isn't what you want, and that Vila has her ring, then what do you call this?" She raised one sharp-arched eyebrow and brought the hoop-shaped weapon close to Mara's face. The thing gave off heat and crackled, like lightning caged.

"I really couldn't tell you," Mara said, swallowing hard. "Except Vila has one almost exactly like it. Hers shone brighter and fizzled like a hot stone thrown into water. This one . . ." she pretended to consider it, ". . . seems pale next to it. How did you come by it?"

Devena stood up and ran her finger along the hoop. Sparks flew and the air seemed to fill with electricity, but the goddess seemed displeased, uncertain. "Veles gave me this. He promised that it would keep my upstart sister in check. That some of her power ran through it and into me."

"Well, if the powerful Veles gave this to you then it must be so." Mara opened her mouth in awe. "Except . . ." She let the words hang there for a moment, longer than was comfortable. Devena's eyes flitted away from the hoop and to Mara's seemingly troubled face.

"Except what?"

Mara pretended to hesitate. "Except . . . *do* you feel more powerful with it?"

"What are you talking about? Of course I do!" But Devena seemed anything but certain now. "I believe I do . . ."

"Well, I only saw Vila with her ring, and she seemed to grow in power every time she held it. The mountains shook when she raised her arm and they crumbled when she brought it down. And this . . ." Mara pointed at the ring, ". . . though doubtless a fine weapon, it doesn't seem to change you in any way that I can see. Unless you were very weak before it had been given to you . . ."

Devena snarled and Mara put her hands up.

"Is it possible?" Devena seemed troubled. She lifted the ring this way and that, inspecting it in the evening light. "Veles wouldn't dare trick me in this way, wouldn't dare give me a fake!"

Mara brought her hand to her mouth, as if she'd never heard such blasphemy. "I'm sure he didn't! There must be another explanation for why he said this was Vila's ring, when Vila has a weapon in her possession right now, much like this and yet much stronger . . ."

"He made a fool of me!" Devena screeched like a bat. "He laughed at me, made me wear a useless bauble! Made me hunt *his* enemies for him! Like I'm his servant, his errand-girl!"

Mara winced.

Devena raised the ring above her head and then, with a fury, flung it into the sky.

The weapon twirled and spun so fast that soon all Mara could see was a sphere of lightning, crackling with electricity and speeding through the air with deadly precision.

A flash of light suddenly blinded Mara, as above them a strong hand grasped the hoop and raised it triumphantly.

"You've kept to your side of the bargain, Mara." Vila smiled above them, her *kokoshnik* shining golden above her head, her braids flowing behind her. "And now I'm free."

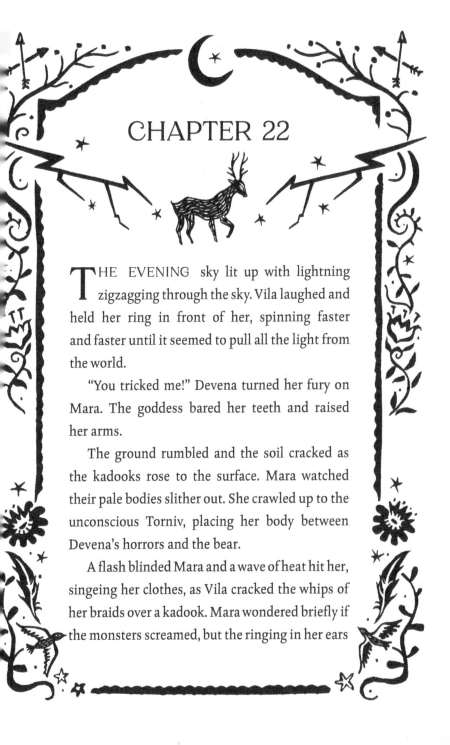

CHAPTER 22

THE EVENING sky lit up with lightning zigzagging through the sky. Vila laughed and held her ring in front of her, spinning faster and faster until it seemed to pull all the light from the world.

"You tricked me!" Devena turned her fury on Mara. The goddess bared her teeth and raised her arms.

The ground rumbled and the soil cracked as the kadooks rose to the surface. Mara watched their pale bodies slither out. She crawled up to the unconscious Torniv, placing her body between Devena's horrors and the bear.

A flash blinded Mara and a wave of heat hit her, singeing her clothes, as Vila cracked the whips of her braids over a kadook. Mara wondered briefly if the monsters screamed, but the ringing in her ears from the first lightning strike made it impossible to hear.

"She tricked you, sister, but *you* betrayed *me*!" Vila landed between the charred remains of Devena's servants. "For centuries, Veles kept me as a servant while you looked on!"

Devena snarled but Mara noticed she didn't try to deny it.

"Mara's done me a service," Vila said, "and for that, you will restore her friends to her."

"Why would I do that?" Devena laughed. "She made a fool of me, sister. She and her friends can rot for all I care."

A tendril of fire travelled across Vila's face. "You have helped chain chaos, Devena. I'm more powerful than you. I'm older than you. And unless you do what I demand, I will stop every hunt. I will burn every predator before their teeth sink into their prey. I will blot out the moon with my fire before a single falcon takes flight. I will still the blood of every hunter alive if it means you're diminished by it." Vila's eyes were the centre of the flame, her burnished gold armour burning brightly, and Mara didn't doubt the truth of her words. Vila would see the world burn and would laugh as its ashes covered the ground.

Mara shuddered. This was a Goddess of Chaos in full glory and a part of Mara wished she'd never been set free.

"Devena, you helped Veles imprison your sister," Mara whispered. The Goddess of the Hunt didn't deign to look at her, but Mara could tell she was listening by the way she kept her face carefully composed. "You hate me now, and

I understand that. But I couldn't have tricked you if a part of you didn't want to be tricked. A part of you wanted to release your sister. A part of you wanted to right this wrong, or you would never have fallen for the lies of a nobody like me."

Devena's face remained impassive, but Mara could feel the goddess calm down by how the fury in her own heart was subsiding. Devena's moods spread like a plague all around her, and Mara knew the goddess wanted to hear what she had to say by how the hunger in her stomach and the itching in her fingers ebbed away.

No god wants to be tricked. Mara didn't allow herself a smile. A smile would be foolish. It could make the goddess suspect she was being tricked again. And she so badly wanted to believe. To believe this had been her choice, really, to release her sister. Her choice to let go of the ring. Her choice, her own, and not Mara's words at all.

"Perhaps so," Devena said, her eyes locked with Vila's. "The child was a tool for both of us. She helped me help you. And I try not to break useful tools." She turned to Mara. "I will offer you a choice, wind child."

Mara winced. *Of course, nothing could ever be easy.*

Devena lifted her hands, palms up, and above each hand a shimmering pearl grew, ever larger, until two orbs hung in the air, their shiny surfaces swirling like ink in water.

"What are they?" Mara made the effort to stand. Her head was swimming and she had to lean against the tree, which still bore the rusty marks of the blood it had scraped off her skin when Torniv collided with it.

"Come closer," Devena smiled. "Surely you recognise this?"

Mara took a step forward. She squinted as the pain in her head pierced needles behind her eyes. The orb on the left was red-hued and whatever was inside it moved lazily. The one on the right was two-tone, like two fish swimming in a bowl too small for them.

She heard it then. A low hum, which matched the rhythm of something deep inside her. She glanced at the smiling goddess. Devena's face had a pleased, focused look. Mara instinctively shrunk away. It was the focus of a hawk about to swoop down on a vole.

The left orb drew her eyes though. And the pain Mara felt wasn't just what she felt in her chest or in her head anymore. She was yearning for whatever it was that swirled around above Devena's hand.

"You have to pick one, and one only, Mara," Devena said.

Mara glanced at Vila, who stood with her muscular arms crossed on her chest. "It's a boon, wind child. You're the only one who can decide which one you choose," said the Goddess of Lightning.

"You're no help," Mara muttered under her breath. She reached out with both hands and hovered her fingertips above each orb. There was something familiar with the one on the right, but the one on the left pulled her and called to her, in a way she didn't understand.

Still, she wouldn't make a blind choice. Devena's gift was a trap, as surely as the sun was hot. Mara closed her eyes and tried to listen to the hum, the vibration of the music which sent a shiver down her spine.

"It's my soul," Mara said, willing the words to be untrue. "My human soul." She opened her eyes and saw the sickening smile spreading across Devena's face, which all but confirmed it. "But that's impossible. I was told it was impossible. My human soul is gone . . ."

"I hunted it down myself, little wind child," Devena said. "I rode on buzzard's wings across the Milky Way and searched for this spark among the stars."

"Why?" Mara's eyes were filling with tears. The empty space inside her screamed at her to reach out, to wrap her fingers around the sphere holding her human soul, hovering above Devena's hand. She didn't move.

"You're Stribog's granddaughter. Veles ripped your soul from you and shouted out in anger so that all who listen could hear. But for all his tricks, Veles was a fool, for he released your soul into the sky, so it could melt into the midnight air and rest: a bargaining chip rendered useless." The goddess wiggled her fingers, making Mara's trapped soul swirl a little faster. "I had planned to sell it to your grandfather, or perhaps to destroy it in front of him to taunt him. I hadn't decided which one. But perhaps you want it instead?"

"You said it's a choice," Mara said. The words were an effort when all she wanted was to reach out and feel whole again.

"Well, yes, as so much in life is." Devena turned to the second orb. "You say you want me to return your friends to what they were before. And I could do this, of course. But the stars will be honoured tonight, and at least one soul will travel across the night sky to melt into the fabric of the world. And it doesn't have to be yours."

The realisation of what Devena meant hit Mara with full force. She looked at her soul and then at her own pale-blue hands. The warmth of her father's bloodline, the link to who she was rested above the goddess's hand. Her human soul moved slowly, sluggishly, as would any mortal soul which had gone through Navia.

For all she'd tried to ignore it, there was an empty space inside Mara's heart. The wind soul that animated her froze her heart and carried her ever further from who she had once hoped to be.

The lack and the longing tasted bitter on her tongue as Mara made her choice.

CHAPTER 23

TORNIV BLINKED slowly, his pupils adjusting to the darkness. Beside him, Vadim lay very still, his human body sleeping off the stag's exhaustion. Torniv saw the crowns of the great trees domed above him, outlined against the moonlit sky.

"Mara?" Torniv said, the panic in his chest growing. "Mara?"

"I'm here," a small voice answered. Torniv turned his head toward the sound.

Mara sat slumped against a tree, her laboured breathing raising her chest with frightening irregularity.

"Mara! What . . ." He stopped suddenly. His eyes went round. "I remember. Oh gods, Mara, I remember everything!" He stumbled over to her and lifted her hand gently. His eyes filled with tears. "I almost killed you! I *wanted* to kill you!"

Mara shook her head. "It wasn't you. Devena filled you with the hunger. I don't blame you. And I'm sure Vadim doesn't either." She nodded at the sleeping figure of Torniv's brother.

"If it wasn't for you, I would have killed my own brother." Torniv pinched the bridge of his nose. "Remind me never to mess with Devena again."

Mara chuckled and squeezed his hand.

"You need a reminder to make you not court death?" Vila's voice rang in their ears. "That's a terrible strategy for a mortal, you realise?" She landed softly beside them, resplendent in her armour.

Torniv glared at the goddess and Mara thought it best to change the subject. "Do you feel all right now?"

Torniv looked pensive. "I think so. All right, but different. I . . ." He held out his hand, the moonlight painting it blue-green. Torniv frowned and his fingernails shifted, elongating, their ridges darkening. Fur sprouted on the fingers, which grew into what was, undeniably, a bear paw.

Mara's mouth hung open. "How is this possible? Uncle Borovy said nobody would be able to control your transformations!"

"Not 'nobody'," Torniv said, as his hand returned to its original shape. "He said 'Not the winds. Not a human.' But Devena is neither of those things. When she pulled my human soul out of me, I could feel things shift inside me. The bear took up more space and I could feel its edges as it gained control. With my soul returned to me, I can still feel the same edges. I think I can call on the bear now."

"And it can call on you," Vila said. "You are more bear now than you were before my sister got hold of you. The bloodlust will live on in your heart, and if you fail to control it, it might take over once more."

Mara considered this for a moment. She looked at Torniv's troubled face and smiled. "He can control it." Torniv gave her a grateful smile and she realised he hadn't been so certain himself.

"We need to send Vadim back to Mama Bohyna," Torniv said.

Mara nodded. "Vila will help us with Koschei, but we've put your brother in enough danger."

"I doubt he'll just go." Mara looked at the sleeping Vadim. Suddenly, her face brightened. She put cupped hands to her mouth and called out.

After a while, Sniezinka emerged between the trees. The deer came up to Mara and lowered her head to sniff at Mara. Mara laughed and embraced the animal's neck.

"I knew you were still around." Mara wiped at her face with her sleeve. "I have one last favour to ask you . . ."

Torniv looked on as Sniezinka trotted away, the sleeping Vadim tied to her back. Torniv took a few breaths and allowed his body to shift itself back to his human form. "Very useful for picking up older brothers, this trick." He laughed sadly.

Mara looked at Vila. "You promised to help us defeat Koschei. Well, I got your ring and your kokoshnik. I think it's time you paid us back, don't you think?"

Vila smiled and nodded. "I think it is." She rose into the air and, holding her twin braids, one in each hand, she slowly lifted them up.

Mara realised a fraction of a second before Torniv. "Torniv, to the ground!"

They both ducked as the lightning crisscrossed the night sky.

"What are you doing?!" Mara screamed, ignoring the pain in her chest. "You're going to call him to us!"

Vila hovered above them, a bright grin on her face. "I promised I'd help you defeat him, little Mara. To defeat him, you have to face him. I'm making you face him and so I'm giving you a chance to defeat him. My promise and my work are done. I wish you luck, wind child." And with that, she shot up through the sky.

The sky was already filling with the ink of Koschei's wings.

CHAPTER 24

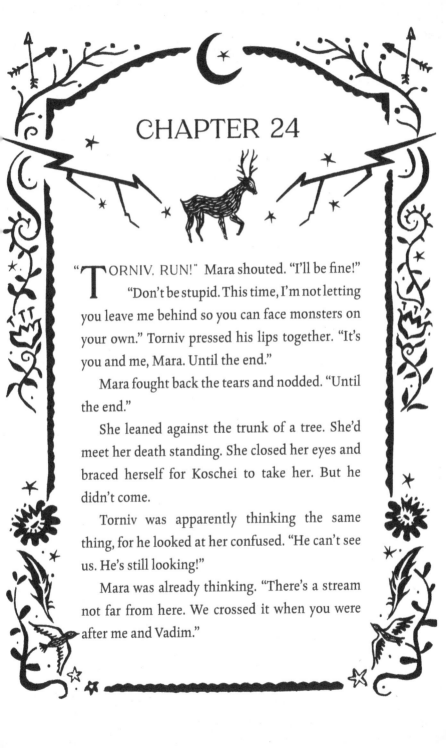

"TORNIV. RUN!" Mara shouted. "I'll be fine!"

"Don't be stupid. This time, I'm not letting you leave me behind so you can face monsters on your own." Torniv pressed his lips together. "It's you and me, Mara. Until the end."

Mara fought back the tears and nodded. "Until the end."

She leaned against the trunk of a tree. She'd meet her death standing. She closed her eyes and braced herself for Koschei to take her. But he didn't come.

Torniv was apparently thinking the same thing, for he looked at her confused. "He can't see us. He's still looking!"

Mara was already thinking. "There's a stream not far from here. We crossed it when you were after me and Vadim."

Torniv winced at that. "I'm sorry . . ."

Mara waved at him to be quiet. "No! *Running water*, Torniv! We can lose him if we find running water! But I can't run!"

Understanding spread across Torniv's face. "But I can!" He stood up straight, looking at his hands, which spread out and grew claws. He raised his face, outlined against the bright moon, and a roar came from deep within his chest.

Torniv-the-bear sat down next to Mara, so she could half-climb, half-crawl onto his back. "Hold on tight," he said, and they were off through the woods.

No birdsong rang through the forest. The animals hid in their burrows and lairs, as a blood-curdling screech got ever closer.

"I need to go faster," Torniv said, and Mara barely had a second to brace herself before the trees blurred at a terrifying speed.

"He's getting closer," Mara whispered, as a black tendril shot out barely a stone's throw away from them, zooming between the trees; searching, searching.

The sound of the stream came through loud and clear, and the narrow ribbon of the cascading water appeared before them.

"Wade in," Mara said.

Torniv grunted agreement as he carefully stepped into the cold water.

"Now what?" he said.

"Now we see how many friends I have . . ." Mara slid off Torniv's back and into the water. The cold didn't bother her, but the slippery stones were a worry. She held on to Torniv for if she fell down she wasn't at all certain she'd be able to get up again. "Can you catch a fish?" she looked to Torniv.

He did the best bear approximation of a shrug.

She looked around. "We need an offering! Something to call Aunt Borova and Uncle Borovy!" She waded through the water, bent double to hold her face close to the water. She squealed with delight and plunged her hand into the icy water. She pulled out a tiny crayfish, condemned by the moonlight reflected in its shiny armour. It was no bigger than her little finger, but it fought bravely, twisting round to close its pincers on Mara's hand. She brought it to the shore and put an end to it, piercing its back with her small knife.

She looked around for some pinecones, but they were surrounded by birches, their bark gleaming pale. Instead, she placed some small pebbles from the stream bed around the crayfish. She had no hair left to bind them. "Please, Aunt Borova, please come . . ."

It took a moment, but the forest was awake and listening and Aunt Borova rose up from the ground, anger burning in her small eyes. "Once more you call us," she said, "and you have nothing more to bargain with either! What gives you the right?"

"Desperation," Mara answered, truthfully. "Koschei will be here in a moment. I don't ask you to stand against him. Just please, use the hair you cut off my head to call Stribog. To tell him I'm trapped. Please . . ."

"So that's what happened to your hair!" Torniv exclaimed. Both Mara and Aunt Borova shot him an annoyed look. He lowered his eyes. "I thought it'd be impolite to ask . . ."

"I won't help you, child." Aunt Borova shook her head. "I cannot step between you and Koschei. My husband and I defend the forest. It is our life and our purpose and the heart of us. I'm fond of you, but I cannot bring the wrath of Koschei upon us because of that."

"The wrath of Koschei is already here,' Torniv whispered, as the ash began to fall.

"Fire!" Aunt Borova brought her hand to her mouth.

"And it's not the fire which renews and heals, Aunt," Mara said. "This is poison, seeping into the ground, rotting the buried seed and killing birds in flight." At a distance, the fire raged, the red aura of it colouring the sky.

"We will call the God of Winter Winds, wife," Uncle Borovy said, striding towards them. He appeared without his companion animals. His wolves and his falcons and buzzards and fawns, all sent away. "Koschei is destruction. We cannot guard the forest from him. And if we do not protect it with all the means at our disposal, then who are we?"

Aunt Borova stared towards the sky, the treetops curling from the heat of Koschei's wings. A starling fell from the sky, hitting the ground in front of her. She leaned down and picked up its lifeless body. She stroked it gently and then lifted it to her lips. A heartbeat later, the starling stirred. It hopped upright, spread its wings and was gone.

Aunt Borova looked at Mara and nodded. She spread out her hands and, between her fingers, strands of silver rose up like wisps of smoke. Mara gasped. It was her hair. In Aunt Borova's hands, her hair rose up like a web, nearly invisible and yet strong enough to capture and call the winds.

It floated up to the sky, strands of silver against the blackness.

The ground rumbled and shook, and the tendrils of ink-like shadow converged on the ground, rising up into the familiar shape.

"I see you, wind child. I see you now." Koschei smiled, the straight panes of his youthful face moving out of sync with the sounds escaping his throat, his black featherless wings folded like a cape on his back. "You have taken longer to find than I'd expected. For which, I thank you." He gave a courtly bow, mockery shining in his dark eyes. "I had nearly forgotten the pleasure of a challenge. Yet all good things come to an end. Alatnir, please." He held out his hand, palm up.

Torniv growled.

Koschei didn't even glance in his direction, but one of the

shadow tendrils snaked its way from beneath his cape and struck Torniv. The force of the blow threw him out of the stream and Torniv cried out as he rolled onto the bank.

Mara stifled a scream. *Calm, you have to be calm.* She turned towards Koschei. "If I give you your soul, you will just kill me."

Confusion crossed Koschei's face. Dark veins momentarily lifted the skin under his eyes, slithering like maggots, until they sank in once again, leaving his face once more like that of a perfect statue.

"Of course I will kill you, halfling. Your death is inevitable, but the means of your death is not yet decided." He showed his teeth again, this time in an unmistakable snarl. "Though the longer you make me wait, the more I lean towards 'excruciating', truth be told." He clicked his fingers and a wall of black fire rose behind him. The ancient trees creaked as the flames slithered up their trunks, splitting them apart.

Aunt Borova screamed and fell to her knees, as the healthy wood turned to rot and dust, feeding Koschei's shadows.

Uncle Borovy, who stood silently behind his wife, cast Mara a mournful look and then seemed to come to a decision. He opened his arms, and, from beneath them, a cloud of insects came buzzing out. A dark, swarming arrow, flying towards Koschei. Wasps, hornets, precious bees. They all attacked in a fury, defending Aunt Borova, their queen and their mother.

"Get out of my forest!" Uncle Borovy screamed, and beetles flew out of his mouth, buzzing with their pincers open. Their opalescent wings created a noise which vibrated across Mara's skin.

Koschei moved his hand in a cutting motion, and the first wave of insects shattered against a pane of shadow.

Tears of mourning poured down the craggy crevices of Uncle Borovy's face, as he lifted his moss-covered foot and brought it down, cracking the ground open. The severed earth split in a jagged line towards Koschei.

Koschei's movements were lazy, as if the strength of the forest's attack was beneath him. His feet shifted in a slow, precise dance, lifting him up and out of danger. But his eyes flashed in anger and he released a wave of darkness which poured over Uncle Borovy.

Mara and Aunt Borova both screamed as Uncle Borovy's long limbs splintered and cracked. The forest shook as the moss and lichen covering his ancient body was torn off, revealing pooling sap. Uncle Borovy's amber eyes turned to his wife as he mouthed a silent goodbye in a language too ancient for Mara to understand.

And then he was gone, the proud Guardian of the Forest, splintered and ground to dust at Aunt Borova's feet.

Koschei now turned to Mara, his anger seemingly spent for a moment. He reached out, his hand still.

"I've been told you were my mother's lover once," Mara

said. She glanced towards the sky where the now-invisible web of her own hair remained as a, so far unanswered, beacon for help which was likely not coming. "Perhaps you love her still?"

Koschei's face shifted. Something like amusement showed in the lifted corner of his mouth. "You're ill-informed."

"You loved her once." Mara hoped it was true, though she had to fake the certitude in her voice. "Killing her only child would not be a good way to honour that past."

Koschei threw his head back and a horrifying yowl came from his mouth. Mara shrunk back when she realised it was laughter. "Your mother threw me aside! She threw away the promise of an immortal alliance, and for what? You? The little worm, pale and powerless? The offspring she chose to bear can't even push the Spring clouds along! Our offspring could have ruled the world! "

"And it still might." A familiar voice came in as a whisper, barely audible over Aunt Borova's keening.

Mara looked up and swore under her breath. Of all the useless creatures to have answered her call for help, this one was the one she wanted to see the least.

"Hello, mother," she said as Zevena flew down on a soft breeze, her pale-blue skin and silver hair shining in the moonlight.

CHAPTER 25

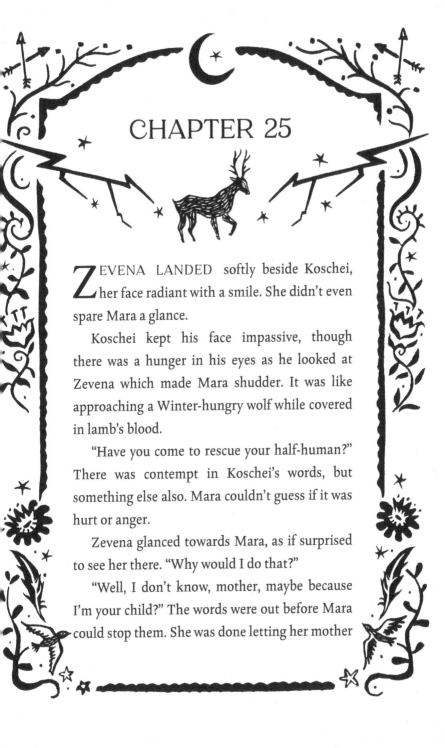

ZEVENA LANDED softly beside Koschei, her face radiant with a smile. She didn't even spare Mara a glance.

Koschei kept his face impassive, though there was a hunger in his eyes as he looked at Zevena which made Mara shudder. It was like approaching a Winter-hungry wolf while covered in lamb's blood.

"Have you come to rescue your half-human?" There was contempt in Koschei's words, but something else also. Mara couldn't guess if it was hurt or anger.

Zevena glanced towards Mara, as if surprised to see her there. "Why would I do that?"

"Well, I don't know, mother, maybe because I'm your child?" The words were out before Mara could stop them. She was done letting her mother hurt her. She knew that. She'd made the decision to not expect love from Zevena, not yearn for her affection. And yet it still surprised her how the indifference on her mother's face had the power to drive ice into her heart.

Koschei eyed Zevena suspiciously. The dark lines lifted once more, swirling underneath his skin as he considered the woman before him. "You are here now, as your child is about to die. Forgive me if I don't find your indifference entirely convincing."

"I've been called by a web crafted from the silver hair of Stribog's kin," Zevena pointed to the night sky. "I had no inkling about their source or that Mara was involved. She has severed the link between us and so has freed me from the burden of her frailty." She waved towards Mara, a dismissive gesture which drew tears from Mara's eyes. "I made a mistake, Koschei," Zevena said, taking a step towards him. "She was a mistake I've regretted since the day of her birth."

"Thanks, mother," Mara said, but was ignored.

"Oh, it was vaguely pleasant at first, I don't deny. But Mara's been my chain and my fetters and it didn't take me long to realise her limitations."

Koschei's eyes were fixed on Zevena. "I warned you. You could have had power with me: real power. Not the weak, limited stuff of your father's winds. Not guarded by the seasons or ruled by the fates. We could have created something more."

Zevena was now only a step away from Koschei, her features softened with the type of affection she'd never shown her child. She lifted her pale-blue hand to Koschei's face and he didn't shrink back. He blinked slowly, as if movement could startle the moment away.

"We still can." Zevena leaned forward and kissed him.

Mara watched, forgotten, her mouth hanging open, as Koschei the Deathless wrapped his arms around her mother, his shadows having fallen soft around them.

"What is that?" Mara whispered. A brightness seemed to light up Koschei. He broke away from Zevena, the dreamy smile that lingered on his lips melting away as his face contorted into a grimace. A swirling gleam moved under his skin, warming the blood in his veins. With a scream, he pushed at Zevena with the combined force of both his arms and his shadow-wings. Zevena's body flew through the air and collided with an oak tree. She slid down to the ground, the tree's roots seeming to embrace her.

She looked up at Mara, berry-blue blood pouring in a trickle from the corner of her mouth. "I took Alatnir, child."

Mara's hand flew to her chest. She pulled the pouch up by the string. She shook its contents onto her palm. A shard of ice fell out, shaped like Alatnir, and already melting against Mara's skin.

"You took it when we met in the Veeray tree!"

"I slipped it in his mouth, Mara," Zevena whispered.

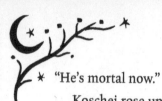

"He's mortal now."

Koschei rose up in the air, the light of his soul gleaming purple and red beneath the thin skin, swirling and wriggling inside him, looking for its place, left too long unoccupied.

"You will pay for this betrayal, Zevena!" he said, struggling to control his voice. "Your halfling child will die now, and you will watch as I tear her limb from limb and peel the skin off her face."

"I think not, Koschei." A flurry of snow and icy wind hit the ground like a whirlpool. Stribog stood before Mara, in his human aspect, his shoulders broad and his beard trimmed short. "You have harmed my daughter." He pointed at Zevena. "My granddaughter had chosen her own path and so if you'd chosen to kill her, I wouldn't have interfered." He glanced at Mara and winked, as if this was a joke between them. "She reaps what she sows that one. But Zevena is mine to protect."

Koschei laughed. He spread his hands wide and a hundred black arrows flew through the air.

Stribog stood still as the wind raged around him, shattering Koschei's arrows. As the God of the Winter Winds and the Deathless One fought, Mara crawled up to Torniv. She placed her hand to his nose and held her breath. She whispered his name and blinked away the tears. He was breathing.

"Wake up, Torniv." She shook him.

A blast of wind hit her, rolling her away from the bear. Stribog and Koschei were well-matched and her grandfather's storm bent the trees around them while Koschei scorched them.

Mara's ribs hurt so much that she wished she didn't have to breathe. She dug her fingers into the soil and pulled herself back towards Torniv.

A silver-blue wisp floated past her face and towards Torniv. It touched him in a gentle caress before spreading in icy needles across his snout. Torniv shuddered and opened his eyes at the same time as a howl rose from deep within him. Mara whipped her head towards Zevena, who smiled at her and sighed, letting her hand drop to her side. Mara wiped her eyes with her sleeve and nodded to her mother.

Mara kneeled by Torniv. "I'm here, I'm here." She put her hand on his nose and they locked eyes.

A crash sounded through the air, as the ice-cold wind blasted them on all sides.

"Is he winning?" Torniv asked. Mara embraced his neck.

Stribog's form shifted, a solid form requiring too much effort to maintain. In one moment, he was an eagle swooping down towards Koschei's uplifted face, then he rose like a mountain under his feet.

Yet, through it all, Koschei never stumbled, his face focused and impassive.

"I'm not sure he can," Mara said, wishing she was lying.

She wished she could say something that comforted her friend rather than the truth that lay before her.

Stribog had as much as told her he couldn't defeat Koschei. And yet he tried.

She held Torniv a little tighter, counting every breath.

Koschei kneeled on the ground and tore at the soil with his nails. The shadow he controlled pooled beneath him, spreading its disease in a dark cloak beneath their feet. Then he stood up, his arms raised in a sweeping motion, as the darkness lifted its edges, wrapping itself around Stribog who had taken on the form of an ice dragon, breathing ice towards his opponent.

Too late, Stribog realised what Koschei was doing and he shot up into the air as a buzzard, but the darkness had already closed over him. Koschei brought his palms together and the shadow contracted, squeezing the life out of the wind within. There was a clap of thunder and, all of a sudden, everything was still. No wind, no breeze. The air felt like a dead thing between them all.

Mara looked up at the smouldering treetops. Not even the aspens quivered against the moon. She closed her eyes, the loss grabbing her by the throat.

The shadows receded into the ground, revealing the figure of Stribog. He tried and failed to assume a face, his body like a bag of water: shapeless, moving, leaking power as it fell apart at the seams. The dark poison was tearing and pulling at the God of Winter Winds.

Stribog crumpled to the ground and turned his head towards Mara. For a moment, he was a man, and then a stag, and then nothing at all. The two blue embers of his eyes were still there, still piercing Mara to the soul.

"Grandfather . . ." Mara mouthed the word, her fingers digging into Torniv's skin.

A sound travelled across the air, and Mara wondered if she'd imagined hearing a laugh as the mighty Stribog, the ancient God of Winter Winds, was there one moment and gone the next.

Koschei leaned against a tree which darkened and cracked at his touch.

"He's tired," Torniv said.

"Not tired enough." Mara gritted her teeth.

There was nothing left. The Deathless One, even rendered mortal, had just defeated a god. He would crush her and Torniv now. And there was nobody else who could help. Nobody to stand in his way.

You reap what you sow, granddaughter. She heard a fading whisper. *And when offered the choice, you chose to remain wholly of the wind.*

She wanted to say she chose to save Torniv, that she didn't reject her human soul, but the words froze in her throat.

She took a breath and her lungs didn't hurt anymore, her bones mending, her bruises fading.

She took another and felt the wind inside her lungs and the air around her, the invisible pull of the currents and the beating heart of the air.

She took a third breath and where there had been a broken child just a moment before, up rose a god.

CHAPTER 26

"YOU'RE HIS heir..." Koschei stood straight, shock and disgust written plainly on his face. "He wouldn't."

Mara smiled, and for a moment she saw herself, as she stood there. It was hard to know where she was, as if her body and her soul no longer needed pairing. "But he did," she heard herself say, and the words seemed to echo beside her, barely tracing the outline of her throat.

"It's impossible!" Koschei shook his head, as if he could alter reality with his outrage alone. "You're a halfling. A nothing. A powerless worm. You can't hold the power of the Winter winds!"

"But I do," Mara said, though the truth of the words didn't make them any less surprising. "Somebody has to."

Koschei raised his arm. "No matter. I killed

your grandfather. And Stribog had a millennia's experience holding these powers. You cannot match him."

"I can't," Mara agreed, her head cocked to the side. "But I don't have to. You see, my grandfather was always alone. He never needed anyone. That's the wind way." She smiled. "But I'm not all wind. And I know when I need help."

A whisper trailed around Aunt Borova, rousing her from her grief. The guardian spirit seemed older somehow, even than her ancient self, but she rose, fury gleaming in her eyes as she lifted her face.

The last of the Autumn leaves went swirling towards the sky, their edges reflecting the moonlight, the precise breeze created by Mara turning them into a thousand blades, slicing through Koschei's clothes and skin.

Mara called into the air and, on their wings, a hundred and more of Stribog's kin, his offspring and his offspring's children, came flying in. Their help and skill, so often spurned by their proud sire, was now demanded by his heir. "My grandfather had many children, Koschei. I was not indispensable to him. But they are all indispensable to me."

The spirits tore and pulled at Koschei, blurring his vision and confusing his senses. Some fell, split open by the shadow blades slicing the air blindly.

Mara smelled the ice and the snow; the piercing, clean pleasure of the cold in her nostrils. *Could she do this?*

Torniv grunted next to her, pushing his bear muzzle under Mara's palm. She nodded and smiled.

Mara focused, her wind family's efforts buying her the time to reach to the edges of her power. She felt it and pulled all of it in. When she finally held the strength of the Winter storms in her hands, she let it all go.

The blast of ice and frost hit Koschei, freezing his skin and body to the bone. A tentacle of shadow tried to slither its way out, but Mara bent her finger and flowers of frost travelled across the dark shape pooling at Koschei's feet.

The wind spirits dispersed as Mara approached the frozen Koschei, standing like a statue, the look of surprise clear on his ice-covered face.

"What will you do?" Torniv asked.

Mara dug into her pocket and closed her fingers around a sphere.

She smiled. "Step away."

And then she threw the last of Mama Bohyna's gifts. It exploded into a thousand shards, piercing Koschei's body, until long cracks appeared in the ice and his body fell down in a heap of frozen blocks.

Torniv whooped and laughed, but Mara didn't join him. She walked up to Zevena, still lying by the tree where she fell. Mara's mother followed her child with her eyes.

"Thank you," Mara said.

Zevena smiled and nodded.

"You . . ." Mara hesitated. "I'm sorry. You loved him . . ."

Zevena laughed and grasped Mara's hand. "There has only been one creature in this world I have ever loved, child. In my own way. Grudgingly. But there was only ever one."

Mara's eyes filled with tears but she didn't pull her hand back. She looked at her wind-kin wreaking havoc and playing in the forest air, their battle already forgotten.

"Do you think I can do it?" she said. "Do you think I can truly be the new Stribog?"

"No," Torniv said, standing a little way apart. "I think you can be the new Mara, though."

Mara looked up as the clouds rolled in across the morning sky. The Autumn rain fell and turned to a flurry of snow around the Goddess of the Winter Winds.

EPILOGUE

THE AIR was cold, but Sorona Gontova waved away her daughter-in-law's suggestion that she might want to go inside to warm by the fire. "There will be plenty of time to sit in the house when the long Winter nights come," she said. Her daughter-in-law nodded respectfully and went off to complete the afternoon's chores in the barn, while her children played in the muddy road.

Sorona Gontova liked to sit like that, her rocking chair creaking rhythmically as she watched the bare branches of the aspens quiver in the wind. She didn't bother to occupy her hands with sewing or knitting as she used to in her younger days. She had earned her rest, though her own nature kept pushing her towards action; to do something, anything, to fill up the hole in her heart she refused to acknowledge.

Now she just looked ahead, and smelled the mossy, wet smell of the late Autumn, mixed with the scent of fresh milk, waiting in a cloth-covered jug for someone to churn it into good yellow butter.

A colder breeze blew in, and Sorona shivered, pulling her woollen shawl closer around her.

"Grandmother? *Babcha?*" A familiar voice rang next to her. Sorona closed her eyes, ordering the tears not to come. It wasn't there. The child was lost. She knew that. In her better moments she almost accepted it. And she would not allow her mind to soften to the point of conversing with a memory.

But it was not a memory that reached out a pale-blue hand, like bilberries dipped in cream. Sorona opened her mouth, trying to say something, a greeting, anything, but the sound came out strangled.

"I went to find da, Babcha," Mara said, gently squeezing Sorona's forearm. "I was going to bring him back, but I failed."

"Oh, child . . ." Sorona's hands shook so badly she was afraid to lift them to touch the beloved, earnest face looking up at her. "I thought you dead. I failed you. I . . ." Her shoulders shook with a sob. "You . . . you look like your ma now." She swallowed, pulling in what reserves of strength she had left. "Your . . . your grandsire will want you now then, I expect? He won't let you stay among us ordinary folk? I will lose you again?" Sorona closed her eyes. She'd been through enough to know she could survive this blow. The child was safe, that was all she could expect.

"My grandfather is dead, Babcha," Mara said, a little sadly, Sorona thought. "There's no Winter Wind but me now." She raised her hand and a beautiful flower of frost appeared above it. She gave it to Sorona, who held it like it was a rabid rat.

"Will you . . . ?" Sorona hesitated. Was it proper to speak so to the God of Winter Winds, even if she *was* your granddaughter? She took a deep breath. "Will you sup with me? Tell me of your adventures?"

Mara smiled. "Anytime I'm welcome."

Mara helped Sorona stand up and they walked inside together.

And for the years to come, many marvelled at the mild Winters of Sorona Gontova's village, which never frosted the Spring bloom of the orchards and never froze a lost lamb in the hills.

And in the long Winter nights throughout Prissan, folk would often tell stories of a girl, blue-skinned and silver-haired, who walked in the moonlight with an old woman on her arm, and with a bear at her side.

ACKNOWLEDGEMENTS

I T TAKES a village to bring forth a book.

Here are the members of my village, to whom I give thanks:

My husband Cameron and my two clever, joyful, kind daughters, Scarlett and Sienna.

My loving and supportive family, in Poland and in the UK.

My amazing agent, John Baker: may his enthusiasm and energy never falter. Also Lorna Hemingway, Sarah McDonnell and everyone else at Bell Lomax Moreton.

My writing buddies, Nadia Idle and Rachael Twumasi-Corson, who keep me disciplined, keep me honest, and give me the support I can no longer do without.

Caroline Hardaker, my dear friend and my Bookish Take channel co-host. Our chats mean more than you know!

Kasia Szafranowska, my friend always, no matter the distance.

Hazel Holmes at UCLan Publishing, for supporting me in completing Mara's story.

Kieran Baker, whose meticulous editorial work and comments I found invaluable.

Nicki Grant, whose attention to detail I can only aspire to emulate.

Becky Chilcott and Alexis Snell for their work on the cover. I loved it from the very first draft, and I feel very lucky to have such talented people produce the artwork for my book!

Alice Natali and Clementine Gaisman from the ILA team for working tirelessly to introduce Mara and Torniv to the readers in the wider world.

And finally, thank you, reader, for picking up this book.

GLOSSARY

* **Kokoshnik** – An elaborate headdress
* **Mamusha** – Mummy
* **Marushka** – Diminutive of "Mara". Many Slavic languages have special forms to change the meaning of a name or any noun really, to express the emotions accompanying the per-son/word. In this case it could be translated as "dear little Mara"
* **Gontova/Gontovy/Gontovna** – Slavic surnames have different endings for the different members of the family. "Gontovy" is for the man. "Gontova" means "the wife of Gontovy" and "Gontovna" means "the daughter of the Gontov family"
* **Izba** – Room (often the largest room in a wooden house)
* **Moya zabka** – My little frog (a term of endearment)
* **Slonechko moye** – My little sun (a term of endearment)
* **Babcha** – Grandma
* **Lament** – A song or poem of grief
* **Voz** – A horse-drawn cart
* **Synek** – Son (diminutive form, literally means "little son")
* **Sniezinka** – A snowball
* **Baba** – An old woman/crone
* **Boyars** – Members of the old aristocracy in Russia
* **Tsarevic** – A prince

HAVE YOU READ MARA'S FIRST ADVENTURE?